Estelle Thompson has written fifteen novels which have been translated and published in German, French, Dutch and Italian, as well as one non-fiction work. She has written for magazines in both the UK and Australia, including *Woman* and *Woman's Weekly*.

She is a retired dairy farmer, and now lives with her brother on his farm in Queensland, Australia.

THE ROAD TO SEVEN-THIRTY

When Brooke Hardwick's handsome and popular young clergyman husband is murdered, she becomes the prime suspect in the eyes of both the police and the residents of the small country town where she lives. But when two balaclava-clad strangers break into her home, violently demanding something her husband had — and about which she knows nothing — she realises there is danger from more than one quarter, and a complex web of mystery surrounds her husband's life and death.

Books by Estelle Thompson
Published by The House of Ulverscroft:

THE MEADOWS OF TALLON
FIND A CROOKED SIXPENCE
A MISCHIEF PAST
THREE WOMEN IN THE HOUSE
THE HEIR TO FAIRFIELD
A TOAST TO COUSIN JULIAN
THE SUBSTITUTE
HUNTER IN THE DARK
COME HOME TO DANGER

ESTELLE THOMPSON

THE ROAD TO SEVEN-THIRTY

Complete and Unabridged

ULVERSCROFT
Leicester

First published in Great Britain in 2000 by
Robert Hale Limited
London

First Large Print Edition
published 2001
by arrangement with
Robert Hale Limited
London

British Library CIP Data

Thompson, Estelle
 The road to seven-thirty.—Large print ed.—
 Ulverscroft large print series: mystery
 1. Large type books 2. Detective and mystery stories
 I. Title
 823 [F]

 ISBN 0–7089–4464–7

Published by
F. A. Thorpe (Publishing)
Anstey, Leicestershire

Set by Words & Graphics Ltd.
Anstey, Leicestershire
Printed and bound in Great Britain by
T. J. International Ltd., Padstow, Cornwall

This book is printed on acid-free paper

1

He was standing exactly where he had said he would be, in the shadows at the back of the church. Where she had asked him to be.

In a small town like Broadfell it wouldn't do for the vicar's wife to be seen in the arms of another man. Especially when it was only a week since the vicar had been murdered.

The young, smiling, handsome vicar who preached such stirring sermons, who was so kind to the sick, so caring toward the bereaved and the troubled, so laughing and joyful on happy occasions like weddings and christenings. Who was loved by his parishioners and respected by the whole town, regardless of creed or the lack of it.

Who, unknown to anyone else, had spent the three years of his marriage to Brooke Campbell slowly reducing her life to some bleak desert where, in the end, fear had stalked, raw and uncompromising.

She had asked Harley to come here at the end of the day — the day of Damien Hardwick's funeral. There were many people who had come to offer sympathy and support in the aftermath of Damien's death.

But only Harley could possibly understand, because he was the only person to whom she had ever told anything of the truth about her marriage.

Brooke's cousin, her childhood playmate, companion of teenage years; they had shared tears, arguments, laughter and dreams. Because he was her cousin he could come openly to the house, later, just as he had earlier attended the funeral, without raising any eyebrows — neither Aunt Elaine's, Damien's father's sister who had flown up from Melbourne to Queensland on receipt of the news and simply invited herself to stay in the house, nor Damien's mother who, Brooke had assumed, would also be staying overnight.

Just for now she needed to have Harley to herself. Needed to hold him, have him hold her, someone she didn't have to pretend to. Someone who knew that, for her, Damien's death was not the beginning of grieving. It was the end of a nightmare.

She didn't know, then, that it was the beginning of another.

She ran to him, flung her arms around him, buried her face against his chest, without passion, just with the desperate need for comfort, for reassurance. He must have understood. His arms went around her,

2

holding her close, as one might hold a frightened child.

'Oh, Hal,' she whispered, using the nickname that was familiar from childhood. 'I'm so glad you're here.'

In the warmth of his wordless, comforting embrace she let all her tangled emotions loose in tearing, shaking sobs. He went on holding her, stroking her hair, until she had cried out her tears and groped for a handkerchief.

He pulled one from his pocket and pushed it into her hand and stepped back. A stranger's voice said quietly, 'I'm sorry. I'm not Hal, whoever he may be. I just hope he's worth the trust you put in him.'

And he turned and walked away into the night, a shadow among other shadows.

Brooke stood numbly, too stunned to think, to even wonder who he was. Then she fled to the vicarage which adjoined the church. Harley Wilson was sitting in a wooden chair on the small veranda, the light from inside the house — where she had left all the lights on — spilling over his fair hair and long frame. He stood up as she stumbled, shaking, up the path, caught her arm and gave her a cousinly kiss on the cheek which all of Broadfell was welcome to see, if anyone had chanced to be looking. The innocence of the kiss was genuine. Their relationship never had been and never would be anything more than a close and comfortable friendship.

'Hi,' he said, smiling down at her as he took the key from her unsteady fingers and unlocked the door for her. 'Sorry about our rendezvous, but I stumbled on a lovers' tryst, and I guess you did too — hence your quick scurry home.'

'Mmm.' She managed a shaky laugh.

So he had seen a stranger comforting her, only he hadn't known it was no lovers' tryst, and he didn't know that she had been part of it. Perhaps because the mistake was so embarrassingly foolish, she didn't enlighten him.

'Hey!' he said with a concerned frown. 'You do need to talk, don't you? Here, come and sit down over here. Is there anything to drink, or was that taboo in the good vicar's house?'

Brooke shook her head. 'Oddly enough, no. Over there, in that cupboard.'

She sank gratefully into a deep, comfortable armchair while he opened a handsome maple cabinet and dealt deftly with bottles and glasses. He put a stiff brandy into her hand and sat facing her, concern in his blue eyes.

'Isn't there anyone staying in the house with you?'

She shook her head. 'I expected there would be, which is why I asked you to get into the cloak-and-dagger stuff of meeting behind the church. Damien's Aunt Elaine has been staying — arrived with luggage and simply settled in. She was the rather large lady in a somewhat striking purple outfit at the service today, if you noticed. A bit ratty, but means well. I thought she'd be here till at least tomorrow, but she took an afternoon flight home.'

'What about his mother?'

'She drove herself up from Brisbane this morning for the funeral, and drove herself back this afternoon. I did think she might stay, but she wouldn't.'

'She must be more robust than she looks. She looks positively frail.'

'I know. I don't think she's well, but when I asked I was more or less told her state of health was not any concern of mine.'

He watched her for a moment. 'You and she never did get along, did you?'

Brooke smiled ruefully. 'I wasn't nearly good enough for her splendid son.' She couldn't keep the undertone of bitterness out of her voice. It was a bitterness she wasn't proud of, not now. She sighed. 'I

5

shouldn't be like that. Whatever else, he was a young man and he is dead. Dead by violence.'

'That doesn't make him any better than he was in life.'

He studied her in silence as she sipped her brandy. At twenty-nine, only a year younger than himself, she had the slim figure, the elfin face, the clear green eyes, the slightly curling dark hair that he remembered.

But there were shadows of fatigue under her eyes, and drawn lines of tension around her mouth. A girl who had laughed a lot, looking as though she hadn't laughed for a long time. He had seen her only a couple of times since her marriage, and he was faintly shocked to see the signs of weary, dragging unhappiness that clearly went back far beyond the evening a week ago when she had come home from work to find her husband sprawled on the floor of his study, a hideous hole blown in his chest and his own shot-gun propped tidily against the wall. From that alone there had never been any question of possible suicide or accident.

'Have you arranged to go to a friend's place, or have someone stay here with you?'

Brooke shook her head. 'Maree Stewart — she's a very good friend — stayed with me the first night. Since then Aunt Elaine has been here, of course. But I won't mind being alone now.'

She stood up and went to close the curtains, almost as if she wanted to retreat into a private world of her own. Then she turned and looked around the room for a few seconds before she went back to her chair.

'I'll be glad to leave this house. It's a house that should be full of happy memories, but for me it isn't. I'm sorry, Harley, to have asked you to delay going home. I needed to talk — desperately needed to talk — and you're the only person I've ever told that marrying Damien was a dreadful mistake. Even then, I've only told you a very little.' She hesitated. 'I'll tell Maree, and Patricia — Patricia Evans. They're both very close friends. I'll tell them, now that it's done, over, finished. But I can't tell anyone else, because naturally everyone thinks I'm grief-stricken, and that's the front I must keep up. I'm shocked, stunned, yes. But I can't feel grief. I should feel some, surely. Perhaps I will, in time. But right now I can't feel anything — except, perhaps, relief.' She looked up at him. 'I guess that makes me sound like some heartless monster.'

Harley shook his head. 'I know you too well to ever think you heartless. What you sound like to me is someone who has had a rough

7

time — much worse than you ever told me.' A look of curiosity sharpened his normally lazy-looking eyes. 'You're not grieving, you say. Yet when you came in just now you'd been crying.'

She smiled faintly, remembering the scene behind the church. 'I let myself get rid of a few years of tears I'd forgotten how to shed — or been too stubborn to do so.'

'So tell me about it, huh?'

She looked down at her hands in her lap. 'Where do you want me to start? I fell in love with the Damien Hardwick the rest of the world saw. Handsome, charming, always there with a ready laugh or a kind word. A girl I've known since high school tried to warn me to stop and think a lot before I plunged into that marriage. It wasn't that she saw the black side of the nice young vicar. She just thought that perhaps I wasn't cut out to be a clergyman's wife. I laughed, of course. But I think she was right, and so at first, when Damien would fly into a rage with me, I felt it was all my fault. And when I'd get upset, he'd apologize, and all the charm would be back, and everything would seem all right again.'

She looked at Harley and sighed. 'Even now, I'm not certain some of it wasn't my fault, in the beginning. Looking back, I know only one thing: I was in love with him, and it took him a while to kill that. But kill it he did. The man I thought he was — that man warranted any woman's love. The man he really was, didn't. For a time I couldn't quite accept that I'd made such a mistake, and I went on blaming myself for things that went wrong. I thought we'd both faced up to the things that made me rather less than conventionally suited to being a vicar's wife. I wasn't an Anglican. I didn't often go to church, though that never meant I didn't have a strong faith, even if it was a bit unconventional.' She paused for a moment.

'I knew little or nothing about the workings of the church, or the parishioners' expectations of me. I intended to go on with my landscaping business because I love the work. I'd taken young Dean Pollock into the business and he was keen and very capable. Damien had assured me he understood all these things and he would never interfere. He said he was happy for me to go on with my own life.'

Brooke made a bitter sound that was half a laugh.

'Almost from the beginning things changed. He began to demand that I give up my work and just devote myself to being the vicar's wife, at least as he saw the role. At times I was tempted to try to fit the mould, just for peace. And I did give time to some church-related work, at weekends and in the evenings. I did go to meetings and I started a games group for young people and helped form a small choir. I helped organize a group to visit people who lived alone, to take them on collective outings — things like that. I think, by and large, people liked me. It meant I worked some jolly long hours, because I wouldn't give up my landscaping work. I felt — Oh, I don't know — almost that it would be a betrayal of myself as an individual. Or you could call it sheer pigheadedness.'

She gave a small, rueful smile. 'Damien began ridiculing me in front of other people. Teasingly, as if it were all a joke — as other people believed it was, I suppose. But it hurt. And gradually, in private, he became not only critical, but more and more abusive. Not physically. He was never violent. But he steadily undermined my self-confidence until I began to avoid doing or saying anything he mightn't approve of, for fear of an outburst of anger. Sometimes he seemed permanently angry with me. Then he'd switch to being all caring and considerate — as long as he got his own way in absolutely everything. The trouble was, often I had no idea what trifle would send him into a rage. He'd always had a hatred of drugs, and it became almost an obsession. Then a day came when he hinted, none too subtly, in front of several people, that I was using hard drugs.'

She stared into space for a moment, and then went on. 'That crushed the last flicker of feeling I had for him. I told him that night that I couldn't go on living with him. We would have to separate.'

A quick shudder ran through her body.

'I expected him to fly into a rage, but he just laughed. He walked over to me and put his hands on my shoulders. That was all. It wasn't even a hard grip. But I was utterly terrified of him.'

Watching her, Harley saw the haunting memory of that fear drain the blood from her face.

'There was something about him,' she said flatly. 'His eyes, I think. I kept telling myself I was being hysterical. This man was a clergyman, a man who totally believed in his vocation. This was my husband. He would never *harm* me. It made no difference: I was afraid of him. I was afraid because I knew, then, with absolute certainty, the thing I had probably subconsciously known for months — there was something very wrong with him. Mentally.'

Brooke paused, looking into distant thoughts. 'He didn't hurt me, of course. Perhaps he felt he'd made the point, because he must have seen I was afraid. He laughed again, and dropped his hands from my shoulders. He said, 'I won't allow you to shame me by leaving me. You won't go anywhere, because if you do, the police will find all that heroin you have hidden. Far too much for your own use. It wouldn't be just a charge of possession. You've been trafficking. You know how long a prison term you'd get?' '

'Brooke!' Harley was staring at her.

She swallowed the last of the brandy and shook her head. 'I told him not to be so stupid; he knew perfectly well I had no heroin and had never touched it. He smiled that lovely smile of his and said, 'But it'll be here when I call the police. I'll see to that. So unless you want to spend a good many years behind the razor-wire, my love, you'll be a good little wife devoted to her husband'.'

She raised her head and looked at Harley. 'Was he bluffing? I don't know. That was three months ago, and in all that time I never summoned enough courage to call his bluff, because I felt he really may have meant what he said, though how he'd get his hands on the stuff I don't know.'

Harley shook his head. 'Bluffing or not, he

was scum to threaten that. I never guessed
. . . But when your marriage was a disastrous
farce at best, why would he go to such lengths
to preserve appearances?'

Brooke said slowly, 'I've spent many
sleepless hours wondering that. In the end,
I'm sure it was simply because he couldn't
tolerate public rejection. If his wife walked
out on him, it would suggest to people that he
was much less than the image of himself he
created for others to see. Perhaps he believed
in the image himself. That delightful façade
hid something — something dark and ugly.
Something warped. I married him because I
was in love with him. I stayed with him
because I was afraid of him. It sounds
impossibly melodramatic. It just happens to
be true.'

He was silent for a long run of seconds.
'Oh, I believe you,' he said heavily. 'I'm afraid
that sort of thing happens more often than
most of us would ever guess.' He hesitated.
'Brooke, do the police have any idea who
killed Damien? Do you have any idea who
killed him?'

'It wasn't likely to be anyone we knew, I'm
sure of that. Just some opportunist thief who
thought the house was empty, I suppose, and
Damien must have heard him and gone to
investigate. I can't imagine anyone wanting to

kill him for any other reason.'

'But someone did kill him, and it was someone who knew where to find his shot-gun. Why did he have a shot-gun, by the way?'

'He used to do some clay pigeon shooting. I suppose he simply kept up his membership of the gun club, and that entitled him to have a licence. But the gun would have been easy enough to find. He kept it in that tall case in the hall, just inside the front door. The case was locked, but the key was hung on a hook on the wall, half behind the case. Any burglar worth his salt would have noticed it.'

Harley nodded thoughtfully. 'So you think an intruder killed him? It was a burglary gone wrong?'

Brooke looked faintly surprised. 'Well — yes. I haven't really considered anything else, because it just seems unthinkable. I mean — it's just the way neighbours talk to the media after someone's been murdered, isn't it? You know, the 'He didn't appear to have an enemy in the world' sort of thing. But in this case it's true. Who could possibly have wanted him dead?'

She stopped, staring at him, shocked.

'Except me,' she said slowly. 'That's what you're saying, isn't it? I hadn't thought of it like that. Oh, God. Do you think I killed him?'

He leaned forward and touched her hand. 'No. I know you too well and I've known you too long. You couldn't kill him. But someone did.'

She said numbly, 'I hadn't ever — wanted him *dead*. I wanted the courage to call his bluff. I wanted — wanted desperately — to be free. And now I have my freedom. Yes. I can see how it could look to anyone who knew the situation between us. But you're asking me to look at the possibility the police might suspect me, aren't you? And they couldn't even guess what our relationship was.'

Harley looked at her gravely. 'Brooke, that might depend on what stories Damien had spread. You say he hinted to other people that you were on drugs. That story alone is one that's sure to have spread. If the people who heard that remark of Damien's hadn't repeated it or even taken it very seriously at the time, in the light of what's happened they're going to remember it and, human nature being what it is, there's a fair chance someone's going to talk about it now. Perhaps feel it their duty to mention it to the police. And even without any direct information that all was not well between you and Damien,

15

don't imagine the police wouldn't count you as a possible suspect. Statistics show a large percentage of murders are carried out by the victim's partner, with or without some kind of justification.'

Shaken, Brooke rubbed her cheek with one hand. 'Yes, of course. I've been utterly stupid not to realize that I have to expect the police to look at me with some suspicion.'

'I'm sorry, old thing. Maybe I wasn't very kind to point it out.'

She shook her head. 'No, no. I'm glad you did. At least if the police start asking some pointed questions it won't come as such a shock.' She frowned, thinking. 'I don't think any wild rumours can have spread, not yet, anyway, because everyone I know has been so kind; full of compassion, I guess, believing I was grief-stricken as well as shocked into numbness. If people had had any suspicions about me, I think it would have shown.'

'What about the police? How have they behaved when they've talked to you?'

'They've been very nice, really. Just asked the routine things, like were there valuables in the house, was anything missing, had Damien spoken of any threats, did I know of anyone who might have a grudge — that sort of thing. The answer to all those was no.'

'Was it a forced entry?'

'No. But the back door was rarely locked, and never when either of us was in the house.' She smiled faintly. 'This is a pretty peaceful sort of small town. Lots of retired people who like the idea of a mountain retreat combined with the convenience of a village, and immune to snow. I never felt any need to lock doors in broad daylight. The front door may have been unlocked as well. I don't remember. I came in the back way, and that door certainly wasn't locked.'

The front doorbell rang, and Brooke gave a little start at the sharp sound, and made a wry face. Harley stood up, but she shook her head.

'I'll go. I imagine it's some kindly soul come to see if I'm all right.'

She answered the bell's summons and came back smiling in genuine pleasure, accompanied by two women about her age — one tall, slim and fair-haired, the other shorter, with curling brown hair — both looking concerned and slightly embarrassed at having interrupted a visit.

Brooke made introductions. 'Maree Stewart and Patricia Evans, my very best friends; this is my cousin Harley Wilson. His family and mine lived near each other when we were children and teenagers. Anything you want to know about my misspent youth, Harley can

17

tell you, though he's probably too much of a gentleman to do so.'

Harley grinned. 'Either that, or he's too afraid of mutual blackmail. I'm glad Brooke has you two girls to look after her.'

'We don't want to interrupt,' Patricia said quickly. 'We just didn't like the thought of Brooke staying here alone, and we weren't sure whether any of Damien's family would be staying. But now you're here, so that's fine.'

He shook his head. 'I'm driving back to Brisbane this evening. I only stayed on for a chance to talk, and now we've talked, so you're not interfering at all. I've an inner-suburban pharmacy which I closed for today, but I'd better be back to open the door tomorrow or I won't have a customer to call my own. And I agree with you absolutely that Brooke shouldn't be here alone.'

He shrugged. 'As far as the shop is concerned I sometimes wouldn't care if I ran out of customers. I think I'm sick of city living. I was born a country boy and I don't think I've ever acclimatized.'

Brooke looked at him in surprise. 'Harley! I didn't know you felt like that.'

He smiled. 'Well, we haven't seen much of each other over the past few years. Anyway, I'm sorry. This isn't the time for me to be

18

airing my small frustrations.'

Maree said casually, 'You could always move to Broadfell if you really fancy country living. Ian Rice's pharmacy here is up for sale. He's retiring. Brooke, have you eaten anything this evening? You're pale as a ghost.'

Brooke shook her head. 'I'm all right. But if Harley must insist on driving back to Brisbane tonight, I'll make coffee for all of us.'

'No, we won't stay,' Patricia said. 'We've intruded on your time together.'

Harley held up his hand. 'Nonsense. In fact, now that you two are here, there are one or two things I'd like your opinion on. Maree, if you know your way around Brooke's kitchen, you and I will get the coffee, and then we can all have a small conference.'

Brooke smiled. 'Maree's quite familiar with my kitchen, and she's an expert on coffee — she has Broadfell's top-of-the-range coffee shop.'

'Is that right? In that case, come on, Maree. You can instruct me in the finer points of coffee making while you tell me about this pharmacy that's up for sale.'

Maree laughed. 'There's not a lot of instruction I can give about instant brew and that's the only kind Brooke and Dam — ' She stopped in mid-word for a shocked fraction.

'The only kind Brooke ever uses.'

They went out, and Patricia put an arm gently around Brooke's shoulders.

'Sit down. You look so weary. And I still feel we're intruding.'

Brooke sank willingly into an armchair. 'No. You're not intruding at all. There were things I wanted to tell Harley. Needed to tell someone, and he's always been like the brother I never had. And he's the only person I've ever told some of the truth to. The truth about Damien and me.'

Patricia said quietly, 'You've been unhappy for a long time, haven't you?'

Brooke looked startled. 'Pat! How — I mean, did it *show*?'

Patricia shook her head. 'Not really. But there have been times when I could see something was wrong. Maybe because I was so lucky with Robert. We had such a special relationship that perhaps I could see better than most people, that's all. Though I think Maree guessed something was wrong, too.'

Brooke clasped her hands together in her lap. 'Poor Maree! I think I alarmed her once, because I more or less told her I was afraid.'

'*Afraid*? Brooke!' Patricia's eyes darkened with shock.

Brooke sighed. 'I'll tell you both, sometime. Maybe tonight. Tell you the things I've told

Harley. It'll be easier, now that I've poured it all out to him. And now — now that I no longer have to keep acting a part.'

Patricia said slowly, 'I guessed that you and Damien weren't happy, and I became sure of it when he was killed. Because although you were terribly shocked — and no doubt you are still in a state of shock — I didn't think you were swamped by grief, the way you would have been if you lost someone you really loved. I think everyone else believed you were in deep grief. But I didn't. I'm sorry,' she added quickly. 'I've no right to make assumptions like that about you and Damien. And it was just my imagination running riot.'

Brooke shook her head. 'No. You're just too perceptive. You were quite right, though I don't know how you guessed. I thought I'd hidden it pretty well.'

'It's just — just that I'd been there, you see. Been down that same road. Lost my husband in one awful moment, even though in his case it was an impatient driver overtaking on a corner and meeting Robert's car head-on. And but for our son, I'd have lost the whole universe. Forgive me, but I could see that it wasn't like that for you.'

Brooke looked at her friend and saw the pain in her eyes, even though six years had blunted it. She almost envied her that pain, because of the joy that had been there before it.

'No,' she said softly. 'It wasn't like that for me.' After a moment she said, 'Where's Cameron?'

Patricia turned away from unbearable memories. 'Gone to stay with one of his mates from school. Theoretically they're helping each other with their homework — one's good at maths and the other at English — but I suspect in reality the new pool-table Harry's parents have just acquired might be getting most of the attention.'

Maree and Harley came in from the kitchen with biscuits and cake and mugs of coffee on a tray, chuckling over some small, shared joke.

Coffee duly handed around, Maree turned to Harley. 'You said you wanted us to hold a conference.'

He nodded. 'I don't believe Brooke should stay in this house. Certainly not alone.'

'That's what we came to convince her of,' Maree agreed firmly.

Brooke protested, 'I won't be staying here for long, anyway. This house belongs to the church, of course, and a new minister will have to be appointed, and naturally he and his family will need the house. I've told the church hierarchy that I'll move out promptly, as soon as I find a place to rent.'

'I'm not talking about something a week or two in the future,' Harley said. 'I'm talking about now. Starting tonight.'

'That's silly! I can't just walk out!'

'Why not? There aren't any pets, are there — cat, dog, bird?'

'No. Damien wouldn't have any.'

'There's at least one motel in town. It was different when you had your aunt-by-marriage staying here. Slightly batty she may be, but she was another person in the house.'

'Brooke is more than welcome to stay with either of us,' Maree broke in. 'I'm on my own, and Patricia just has Cameron.'

Brooke looked steadily at Harley. 'Hal, I'm not afraid to stay here alone.'

'Then you damn well should be. You say you believe Damien was killed by someone bent on burglary. If so, it was someone perfectly willing to kill anyone who got in his way. Someone who armed himself with Damien's shot-gun just to make sure he wasn't thwarted.'

'Or recognized,' Patricia suggested.

'Or recognized,' Harley agreed. 'But you say nothing's missing, and the house wasn't ransacked.'

'Certainly as far as I know, nothing's

missing,' Brooke said. 'The police asked me to go through the house with them. There was no sign of anything having been disturbed, and I couldn't miss anything. But a shot-gun makes a pretty vicious noise. Whoever fired it would have guessed it would be heard and someone might have come to investigate. Or he could have been so shocked by the realization of what he'd done that he simply panicked and bolted.'

'He must have considered the possibility of killing someone when he took the gun out of the cabinet and loaded it,' Harley pointed out.

Brooke said grimly, 'The idea of shooting someone and the reality of what it looks like would be two very different things for most people.'

Harley looked at her, his face softening as he thought of the fact that she had seen, and would go on seeing in memory all her life, the result of that shot-gun blast.

'I'm sorry, kiddo,' he said gently. 'I'm sounding heartless, putting you through this.'

She gave him a small smile. 'You're sounding like a cop. It's all right. Go on.'

'The point I'm trying to make is that an opportunist, spur-of-the-moment burglary is most unlikely. So unless it was someone with the most fearsome grudge against Damien

— and you say yourself you can't imagine that it was so — then it was someone who wanted something in this house so badly that he was prepared to kill for it. And because nothing was disturbed, it appears he didn't get it, whatever it was.'

There was a silence, while they all realized the implications of what Harley had just said.

'And if he didn't get it,' Maree said, 'there's a fair chance he'll come back. That's what you're saying, isn't it?'

'That's what I'm saying. Now, I've an hour's drive ahead, and I'm not leaving this house, Brooke, until you pack a bag and go home with one of these girls. So be considerate to your poor, ageing cousin and humour him so he can go home and get some sleep.'

Brooke smiled, then gave a little shiver. 'All right, you win. I admit I hadn't really thought it out like that.'

'Right,' Patricia said firmly. 'Then go and pack your toothbrush while I wash these coffee mugs, and Harley and Maree can see to locking doors and windows.'

2

In the end, she went to stay with Maree, though she explained over all protests that she needed to go back to the vicarage each day, in order to be there to answer the phone, deal with mail and begin the daunting task of sorting and packing. She had told Dean Pollock, her young partner in the landscaping business, that she would take a week off work to prepare for the inevitable move to somewhere else to live. She would take only her own personal possessions. She had offered Damien's belongings — books, desk, gold watch, music tapes and CDs — to his mother, who had flatly and emphatically declined them, saying she had no time for sentimental souvenirs of someone else's life.

Brooke paused for a moment in the midst of packing books into a carton, and thought about the thin, wiry, sharp-tongued, keen-brained woman who was Damien's mother. Brooke had never understood Rachel Hardwick, never been allowed past the frosty manner to get to know the woman behind the watchful, pale blue eyes. Mother and son had had a close and profoundly affectionate relationship. Brooke was left to conclude that it was Rachel's jealousy which shut her out, a jealousy directed not so much at her personally as a jealousy which would have been directed at any woman who took over first place in Damien's life.

Rachel Hardwick was a woman who kept her emotions in rigid check. A stranger, observing her yesterday at the funeral of her only child, would have thought she felt no grief at all. Brooke, who knew how much she had adored Damien, knew that the frail-looking, immaculately groomed, stony-faced lady was suffering a grief of untold agony. But when she had tried to offer sympathy it had been icily rejected.

Brooke sighed and resumed packing.

In mid-morning the police came.

Detective Sergeant Harold Thorpe, who had come on that first evening, following hard on the heels of the uniforms, was a quietly dressed man of early middle age and of generally forgettable appearance, except for his intense brown eyes and a curious stillness which made Brooke think of a cat waiting with patient concentration at a mouse-hole.

She said, as she waved the two detectives to chairs, 'I saw you at the funeral yesterday.' There was a hint of puzzlement in her tone.

I wondered why you were there, she thought, a tight knot clutching at her stomach muscles, and I wonder now why you're here, or perhaps I know.

'You were very observant, in the circumstances,' Sergeant Thorpe said without emphasis.

'I was surprised, that's all.' She hesitated. 'I've heard there's a theory that sometimes a killer will attend his victim's funeral. Is that why you were there?'

'It's been known to happen.'

'Do you think my husband's murderer was there, yesterday?'

'Quite possibly.' The tone indicated that the subject was closed. He nodded at his companion. 'You've met Detective Hanson, haven't you?'

'Yes.' She smiled at him and received a friendly grin in return.

Detective Hanson was tall, fair, blue-eyed and good-looking, with a disarmingly cheerful manner. She wondered fleetingly whether it was deliberately cultivated to put people off guard.

His sergeant said, 'I apologize for the intrusion, Mrs Hardwick, but I'm sure you realize we have to pursue enquiries in every avenue. Some of the things we'll ask, you may probably have answered already, but

28

sometimes things become clearer in one's mind with time.'

Brooke nodded, and thought: and what you really mean is that guilty people who have lied may trip themselves up. She said, 'I understand, though I'm afraid I won't think of anything useful.'

'Well, we'll just go over things again. What time did you come home?'

'Shortly before six.'

'Mmm. Then at this time of year it would be virtually dark. Are you usually as late as that coming home from work?'

'No, not usually, but it's not so very unusual, either. I'd been down to a housing development at the coast where we are tendering for some street-front landscaping.'

'Will you tell us exactly what happened when you came home?'

She looked at the wall and saw again, not the wall, but what she had seen that evening, and reflected that there would be many dark nights in her life when her mind would replay it all over again, no matter how she tried to put it aside.

'I put the car in the garage and locked it. I'd bought some milk, and I took it into the kitchen and put it in the refrigerator. There were no lights in the house, so I assumed my husband must be out.'

'Was the door locked?'

'No. It seldom was — never when either of us was at home.'

'You say you assumed your husband was out. Yet surely his car must have been in the garage?'

'Yes. But he could have been anywhere within walking distance.'

'Of course.' He waited.

'I had turned on the lights in the kitchen, and as I went through to the bathroom to wash my hands before I began preparing dinner, I turned on the hall light. Some light from that spills into the study, and the door was open, as it usually was. I could see something on the study floor. I didn't know for a moment what it was, so I went in and turned on the study light.'

She hesitated. It's only words, she told herself; just say them; you don't have to see. But of course she did see it all again in her mind. The detectives waited. She thought they could have made it easier. Not waited for her to tell them of the next couple of stunned, shocked, disbelieving minutes.

'For a moment I didn't realize what had happened. My first thought was that he must have had a heart attack or a cerebral haemorrhage. He was lying sprawled, half on his side. I went to him, and of course I saw there was blood on the floor and as I bent down I saw the front of his shirt. I suppose I knew beyond question he was dead, but — maybe by some kind of instinct that can't accept the unthinkable — I bent down to check his pulse. He — was cold, of course.'

She stopped, remembering. When the police had finally finished with the room, two men who were regular parishioners of Damien's had come and taken up the study carpet, scrubbed the floor and put new carpet down. They had done it quietly, matter-of-factly and unasked, and she would love them forever for it.

'Mrs Hardwick, I know this is all very difficult for you,' Sergeant Thorpe said. 'But did you touch anything in the room?'

'I used the telephone to call the police.'

'Did you pick up the gun or the empty cartridge shell?'

She shook her head. 'No. I didn't even notice the gun at first. It was only after I had phoned the police that I saw it. I didn't see the shell at all. I didn't even think of it. Wasn't it still in the gun?'

'No. Nor anywhere in the room. Did anyone else come into the house before our officers arrived?'

'No. I didn't phone anyone else. Not then.'

'Where was the shot-gun when you saw it?'

31

'Standing propped against the wall near the door.'

'So you would know immediately that your husband hadn't committed suicide.'

Brooke stared at him. 'I never for a moment thought he might have. It simply wasn't in his nature.'

The sergeant nodded. 'So you knew your husband had been murdered. Did you then, or do you now, have any idea why?'

She said slowly, 'I just assumed then that it was a home invasion that went horribly wrong.'

'And now? What do you think now?' He sounded conversationally interested. He might have been asking why she thought the local football team had lost their last match.

'It doesn't make sense.' She thought of the conversation with Harley the previous evening. 'Nothing appears to have been stolen. The house wasn't ransacked.'

Detective Hanson looked up alertly from the notebook he'd been scribbling in.

His sergeant said unemotionally, 'You say nothing *appears* to have been stolen. Surely you would know if something was missing?'

'I mean,' she said, meeting his intense gaze steadily, 'that if something was stolen, it was something I didn't know existed.'

'Did you or your husband own something

of considerable value which someone might have *expected* to be in the house, but wasn't, at the time?'

'Something valuable enough to kill for?' she asked drily. 'No. I have no jewellery, apart from my wedding- and engagement-rings and some quite valueless costume jewellery. My husband had a gold watch and a wedding-ring. And of course there were things like a TV, a stereo, CDs, that type of thing. That's all. No family heirlooms, no secret hoards of cash.'

'Mmm. Did you or your husband use drugs?'

'Certainly not.' She hoped her voice had been as steady as it was indignant, and that the jolt of shock had not shown in her face. Someone had talked about Damien's hint that she was an addict. She wondered just how far that rumour might have spread.

Sergeant Thorpe let several seconds run by. 'Had your husband ever spoken of being threatened by anyone? Or spoken of anyone who might have a grudge, however imaginary, against him?'

She shook her head. 'No. He was very popular in the community.'

'So we gather. But a clergyman must learn all manner of things about people — perhaps things people would prefer didn't become known.'

Brooke said with a faint smile, 'He was an Anglican, Sergeant, and a fairly liberal one. He didn't hear confession.'

'Not officially, no. But people would tend to confide all manner of things to him, wouldn't they?'

'I'm sure they did. But he never told me of anyone's secrets that were told to him in confidence. He wouldn't do that.'

Harold Thorpe simply sat still, watching her. 'A clergyman, particularly a young and good-looking clergyman, can sometimes appear highly attractive to the ladies of his congregation.'

She looked at him with a flicker of genuine amusement. 'Certainly. I'm sure Damien had his share of admirers, with possibly one or two married ladies included. I don't think that explains his murder, Sergeant. I really can't see any of the ladies of Broadfell — or any jealous husbands, for that matter — carrying out a crime of passion over Damien or anyone else.'

'Unfortunately it isn't always possible to know who will murder if the circumstances are right. Would you be confident he was never involved with any other woman? I'm sorry to be asking such a question.'

'I'm sure. Never since we were married

— or engaged, for that matter. He valued his good name, his reputation, both within the church and outside it, far too highly to risk the least scandal.'

If the detectives heard the bitterness behind the words they gave no indication of it, except perhaps by the next question.

'Were you and your husband on good terms? Would you call your marriage a happy one?'

Brooke understood suddenly that this was where the questioning had always been directed. Her senses sharpened at the awareness of danger, just as though the danger had been a physical threat. A typical August west wind had sprung up outdoors, she noticed for the first time. It will blow the last blossoms off the peach-trees in the garden, she thought irrelevantly. Yet somehow the thought seemed to be linked with danger, and the destruction of something innocent. If you were once suspected of murder, could you ever again look at life with confidence?

Her eyes didn't waver from the policeman's, and there was only a fractional pause between his question and her answer.

'No, Sergeant,' she said quietly. 'I would not call our marriage a happy one.'

A tiny flicker of his face muscles suggested that, though she was sure he had suspected it was the truth, it wasn't the answer he had expected.

'Would you like to tell me?' It was the first time his tone had been anything but impersonal, but now it was gentle, almost as if he were about to hear something he wished wasn't true.

'I didn't kill him,' she said. 'But I can't prove it. As for our marriage — I was in love with him when I married him. Perhaps he was in love with me. But I found that Damien was not what he seemed.' She paused. 'No, that's not exactly right. More accurately, he was not *always* what he seemed. Sometimes he would be as charming to me as he was to everyone else. But there was another side — vicious, irrational. He wasn't violent, physically. But he was — I suppose as nearly as I can explain it, he was psychologically abusive. Under the delightful person the world saw, there was something ugly. Twisted.'

'Something rotten in the State of Denmark,' Detective Hanson quoted softly. She flung a quick glance at him, but there was nothing mocking in his expression. He looked as if he understood.

'Yes,' she said. She thought Shakespeare would have understood also.

Sergeant Thorpe was sitting relaxedly in

the easy chair, exactly as he had been from the beginning of the interview. He might have been a friend, dropped in for a cup of coffee and a chat. Except for the nature of the chat.

'Between telephoning the police and the arrival of the first officers, what did you do?'

'I went and got a blanket and laid it over the body. I'm not entirely sure why. It just seemed the right thing to do. And then I simply sat in a chair in the study, and waited.'

'It would have taken the first uniformed officers around fifteen minutes to get here. And you sat in the study for all that time?'

'Yes.'

'You thought your husband had been killed by a thief who had come into the house, yet it didn't occur to you to go and see what might have been stolen, or what damage had been done?'

'Sergeant,' Brooke said with an edge of anger, 'my marriage may not have been a happy one, but a man who had been my husband for three years had been killed. If other damage had been done, it was insignificant by comparison. It may seem strange to you, but it seemed to me simply an act of common decency to stay with Damien's body until the police came.'

Sergeant Thorpe watched her for a few moments without comment, then simply nodded. 'When our officers came, you let them in by the front door?'

'Yes.'

'Was it locked?'

She shook her head. 'I honestly can't be sure, but I don't think so.'

'So your husband may very well have known his killer and may have unconcernedly admitted him. Or her.'

'He may have opened the door, or it may not have been locked, in which case anyone may have simply walked in. Often when my husband was working at his desk, writing letters, or his sermon for the next Sunday, he would have music playing on the stereo, in which case he wouldn't hear anyone come in.'

Detective Hanson flipped some pages of his notebook. 'The stereo system in the study was in fact switched on and a tape in the tape deck had been played, and several other tapes were placed on top of the system, suggesting they had been, or were to be played. When I checked the position of the volume control I found the music would have been reasonably loud.' He added quickly, 'Not loud enough to suggest it may have camouflaged the sound of raised voices, let alone a shot-gun blast, of course, but very probably loud enough to cover the sound of the front door opening. Or the removal of the gun from the cabinet, for that matter.'

Detective Hanson, Brooke reflected, was thorough, and sharply intelligent.

'Assuming that the tape was still playing at the time, it would have indicated to a casual thief that there was someone in the house. Open door or not,' Detective Hanson went on, 'most thieves would be exceedingly reluctant to enter, in broad daylight, premises in a suburban street where someone is at home.'

'Whoever it was,' Brooke said grimly, 'took out insurance against being caught. If theft was the objective.'

'By taking the shot-gun out of the cabinet and loading it? Which, incidentally, would make him a very observant thief, as well as a desperate one,' the sergeant remarked. 'First, he had to be curious about the contents of a polished timber cabinet which could reasonably be assumed to be a bookcase. Then he had to note the key hanging partly out of sight behind the cabinet, and this would have to arouse his curiosity to the extent that, far from making a rapid search for cash or easily sold items like cameras or videos or jewellery, he took time to investigate a locked cabinet — even though whoever was in the house might have come across him at any moment.'

Brooke rubbed a hand over her face. 'I know. I've already told you that I no longer believe it was a casual thief.'

'So you have.' Sergeant Thorpe nodded. 'Mrs Hardwick, how many people would have known where the gun was kept? Or even that it existed?'

She shook her head. 'I really don't know. Probably some of the men in Damien's congregation, because some of them belong to a gun-club and Damien used to go clay pigeon shooting regularly. Not so often lately. I suppose I've mentioned the gun to one or two people. It's just something that's always been there and I simply took it for granted and never thought much about it.'

'Do you know how to handle a shot-gun?'

She felt her stomach muscles tighten with something very close to fear. 'Yes, certainly,' she answered steadily. 'I grew up on a farm. My father taught me to shoot.'

Still without moving from his relaxed position in the armchair, Sergeant Thorpe said, 'Where were you last Friday afternoon between two-thirty and six o'clock?'

Brooke could feel the thudding of her heart, hear the pounding of her own pulse. This can't be real, she thought; this isn't happening.

'I was in the office of the landscaping

business I run with Dean Pollock
— Greenlands Landscape and Garden
Service out on Miller Road — for a time
after lunch.' She made herself speak evenly,
made herself think carefully. It was essential
she recall details as clearly as possible. They
were going to check every word she said.
And, she had a sickening feeling, anything
she couldn't prove, they were not going to
believe. And there undoubtedly would be
large chunks of time for which she had no
witnesses.

'Dean was around the yard for a while,' she
went on, 'loading some materials for a job he
was going to. He left about two o'clock, I
should think. I had a phonecall from a
swimming-pool company — we do any
landscaping for them around the pools they
install. I think that was after Dean left, and
soon after that I drove down to the coast, to
the Blue Crystal Waters development. The
developers are keen to put in extensive street
and footpath landscaping and have called for
tenders for design and practical work
— supply and planting, stonework or
whatever the overall plan requires.'

'And you arrived at the site — when?'

'About two-forty-five, I suppose. I didn't
check the time.'

'But you had an appointment with

someone from the developers, to meet on the site?'

I'll take a bet you already know the answer to that, Brooke thought.

'No,' she said levelly. 'That wasn't necessary at this stage. I simply did a lot of walking along the roadways, looking at the new canals which have been dug, making rough sketches, taking photographs. The intention was that Dean and I would look at the plans — the survey plans of the site — and at the preliminary landscaping ideas I had, and discuss the best approach to try to ensure a fair level of privacy to future residents while making it visually and environmentally attractive.'

Just for a few fleeting seconds the memory of the way the project had caught her enthusiasm pushed the grim present aside, and it showed in the animation of her voice.

'And who would have seen you there as you took photographs and made sketches?' Harold Thorpe asked with apparently no more than polite interest.

She looked at him, trying to seem calmly unperturbed. 'No one who would know me. Some of the men operating the earth-moving machinery may have seen me. I've no idea if they'd remember.'

Sergeant Thorpe glanced at his junior, who

42

again flipped some notebook pages and said, 'An excavator operator remembers seeing a woman with what he called a large notebook.'

'My sketch-book.' Brooke nodded.

'He says you didn't get there until at least three-thirty, probably four or even later.'

Brooke stared. 'But — look, he mightn't have seen me until about that time, but it's a fairly large area, and I drove to various parts of it. There weren't workmen in every section.'

'Of course.' Sergeant Thorpe stood up suddenly. 'Mrs Hardwick, do you mind if we have a look through the house again? I know this has all been done once, but we'd like to go over it again, if you've no objection.'

'Of course not.' Her voice sounded, to her ears, as dazed as she felt. 'Do you want me to come with you?'

'Please.' Detective Hanson smiled disarmingly. 'It's just routine stuff, Mrs Hardwick. We need to know more about your husband — especially whether he had any papers, letters, that sort of thing — things that might seem quite unimportant, but to someone they might be something to be suppressed.'

As she went silently, numbly, from room to room with them, she realized they were looking for more than papers and letters.

43

They were looking, perhaps not surprisingly, for drugs.

Feeling sick, she wondered whether in fact Damien had possessed the heroin he had threatened to produce for the police if she left him. But, though they probed with great care and efficiency — and a minimum of disturbance, for which she was thankful — they found no drugs.

But in Damien's study they found something which interested them keenly. In addition to the engagement diary he kept on his desk, and which gave no hint as to whether he had been expecting a visit from someone on the afternoon of his death, they found, pushed to the back of one of the desk drawers, a small book.

They spent so much time reading it — Detective Hanson looking over the sergeant's shoulder — that Brooke eventually asked, 'Is there something wrong?'

Sergeant Thorpe seemed to consider for a minute. 'Did you know your husband kept a diary?'

'Yes. His engagement diary.'

'Mmm. This is another diary, a personal one. Most of the entries are perfectly innocuous — the weather, small happenings, comments on people he knew, sometimes comments on national events, that sort of thing. However, a couple of months ago — no, longer than that.' He turned back pages. 'Mmm. Mid-April. He wrote 'Brooke is having strange mood-swings, unlike her.' Then a week later, 'Brooke's emotional problems no better.' And so it goes on, 'B. seems better this week — more stable . . . Brooke very depressed but won't talk about it, just gets angry.' These remarks are scattered through the diary, sometimes the only entry, sometimes mentioned with other things.'

He handed her the diary and she turned the pages with shaking hands and a sense of disbelief. The entries concerning her were irregular, written with apparently increasing concern, claiming to have urged her to see a doctor, and always commenting on mood-swings, until, only a week before his death, he had written, 'I can only think Brooke is on drugs. I've tried for so long not to believe it, but I can't see any other explanation.'

Then the rest of the pages were blank.

Very slowly she raised shocked eyes to the sergeant and handed the diary back.

'It's not true.' Her voice was barely above a whisper. 'None of it is true. Ask — ask anyone — Dean, my business partner — my friends — anyone. Ask them about my supposed mood-swings, my erratic behaviour. He was lying.'

A swift surge of anger blazed through her in the wake of shock, and strength came back with it.

'Someone has already told you, I have no doubt, that Damien suggested, in front of several people, that I used hard drugs. At the time they laughed, thinking he was making a joke. But now he's been killed, and someone's not sure it was a joke. That's true, isn't it?'

The two men simply looked at her. Two cats at the mouse-hole now, she thought bitterly.

She took a deep, steadying breath, and told them quietly that she had told Damien he had taken the last step to destroying their marriage, and she would leave him. She told them of his threat, and of her fear of calling his bluff.

Neither detective showed a flicker of what he might be thinking.

'If, as you say, Mrs Hardwick,' Sergeant Thorpe said calmly, 'your husband's threat to incriminate you was totally false and solely designed to protect his image, how do you account for these entries in his diary?'

She shook her head. 'I can't. I can only tell

you he was lying. I have never touched hard drugs in my life. He never urged me to see a doctor. He lied the day he hinted to people that I was on hard drugs. He lied when he wrote those diary entries. He must have had a reason. I don't know and can't imagine what it was, since obviously none of it was designed to drive me away.'

'Mrs Hardwick,' Detective Hanson asked interestedly, 'what was the date of your husband's birthday?'

Brooke stared at him. 'The twelfth of March. Why?'

'I just wondered.'

After a moment the sergeant asked, 'Are you claiming that your husband was mentally unbalanced?'

'Definitely not in the sense that he didn't know what he was doing. I know I said there was something, some personality kink — a quality of *malice*, I think is the best way to describe it, and yet that isn't exactly right, either. Menace might be a word that fits it better. But he would certainly know exactly what he was writing in that diary and he would know it was entirely false. I can only believe there was a deliberate purpose in writing it. I have no idea what that purpose was.'

'Do you think your husband himself used

47

drugs or was in any way involved in the drug scene?'

'No, certainly not. Of that, I'm absolutely sure. He abhorred drugs. He spent much time around schools, talking to students about the dangers of experimenting with even marijuana.'

The sergeant seemed to think for a moment, then nodded. 'You don't mind if we keep the diary for a while?'

'Of course not.' She looked at him squarely. 'You think I killed Damien, don't you?'

Harold Thorpe smiled suddenly. 'We're paid to collect evidence, Mrs Hardwick, not to jump to conclusions.'

He walked back to Damien's desk, sat in the chair facing the desk, then turned his head, stood up, and walked four or five paces, then stood as if lost in thought. Presently he nodded and said, 'Yes. Well, I think that's all for the moment, Mrs Hardwick. Thank you for your help.'

Brooke walked with them to the front door. 'Can I ask whether anyone heard the shot?'

'A couple of people say they heard what they thought might have been a shot, but didn't take a great deal of notice, it seems, because a car backfiring was more probable.

There's some earth-moving machinery working on that vacant site down the side-street, as you would know, so there's a good deal of noise from there. The two houses on the other side of the vicarage from the church were empty — occupants at work. A pity the school over the road was closed for the holidays, because children don't miss much. Still,' he added cheerfully, 'we may yet find a small boy who was riding his bicycle past at the time. Small boys on bicycles know most of what happens in a town this size.'

And with a benign smile that gave no hint as to whether that last remark was simply an observation, or a veiled threat, he picked up his hat from the hall table and the two policemen walked out to their car.

Brooke closed the door behind them and went shakenly out to the kitchen and simply sat on a stool and stared for a time at the wall.

She didn't notice that the detectives sat in their car for a time before they drove away.

★   ★   ★

'Is she right, Sarge?' Detective Hanson asked as he slotted the key into the ignition. 'Do you think she killed him?'

Thorpe gave him a flicker of a smile and

49

fastened his seat-belt. 'Meaning you don't? Or at least don't want to?'

Hanson grinned. 'You just said yourself, Sarge, that we're paid to collect evidence, not to rely on intuition. But there's something odd about that diary. I think it's some kind of fake. I believe her on that score, at least.'

The sergeant raised an eyebrow. 'A fake?'

'I don't mean that he didn't write it. It's his handwriting, to judge by all the other samples there are. But look there, at that date, March twelve. He writes of that motor accident along Norbridge Road, where those two people were killed — says he attended the scene that day.'

Sergeant Thorpe read where the younger man pointed. 'So? It wouldn't be unusual for a minister to go to a thing like that, to offer whatever comfort he could.'

'It's the wrong date. It happened two days later, the fourteenth.'

The sergeant shrugged. 'An easy mistake to make: hadn't written up the diary for a few days, went back to fill it in, and simply put it on the wrong page.'

'Not really. See there, earlier on the same page he writes that it was his birthday, and it's the right date for that. I asked Mrs Hardwick — remember? He wouldn't make the mistake of thinking the accident occurred on that day, because if you read the entry he says, 'Some of the church ladies gave me a surprise afternoon tea for my birthday today, from two till four — sounds dull, but it was quite fun.' That accident happened at just before three.'

The sergeant sat looking at the diary with a frown. 'I — see,' he said eventually. 'So if the diary has such a major mistake, the chances are that it was all written quite recently. And if so . . . '

'If so, it's highly likely it was designed to help point the 'she's a drug-addict' finger at Mrs Hardwick. Falsely.'

'Mmm.' The sergeant considered. 'You may well be right, and she is telling the truth. But if their marriage was unhappy, why should he resort to a threat like that to keep her with him? Oh, I know, I know — we've met up with too many cases where a fellow will *kill* his partner rather than let her go, no matter how unhappy the partnership may be. But not usually clergymen. There's another angle, of course. He faked the diary to give weight to the drug-addict bit simply because the addiction is the truth.'

'It's still very odd behaviour. I don't think the charming vicar was quite what he seemed. There had to be some kind of psychological twist in his make-up. If any

51

half-way decent man believed his wife was a drug-addict, or in some way mentally disturbed, anyone — let alone a clergyman — surely would have tried to get expert help, not just made notes in his diary. And if he *didn't* believe she had a problem, and just wrote lies, either he was hallucinating or he was planning something nasty against her.'

Harold Thorpe sat silently for a while, simply looking at the diary. 'Yes,' he said presently. 'Well, we'll show this to the boss to see what he thinks. But you know, David, whether the diary entries are genuine or not doesn't change the degree of probability that she killed him. She was unhappy. She was at least to some degree afraid of him. She probably had reason to be. That adds up to a reason — right or wrong — to decide to strike first. Let's drive down the main street one block and take the side-street that runs behind the church.'

David Hanson drove as directed and stopped a hundred metres down the side-street. A park and the town's public swimming-pool took up most of the block behind the church and vicarage.

'Mrs Hardwick could have come back here before she ever drove down to the coast. She could have parked in this street about where we're parked now, and walked unobserved across the park, into the vicarage garden. The trees all around would act as a screen,' the sergeant said. 'There's no one at the pool at this time of the year. She could walk into the house, take the gun from the cabinet, shoot her husband and leave again unnoticed.'

David Hanson nodded. 'Yes, she could. So could anyone else.'

'True. But she had some degree of motive — a pretty strong degree of motive. So far we haven't found anyone else who had, or even might have had.'

'She could have worn gloves, of course, which would account for the absence of prints on the gun and the cabinet. But why take the empty shell out of the gun?'

'My guess is that whoever fired that shot didn't wear gloves. There were no prints at all, on the gun, or the key or the cabinet. Gloves would have smudged other prints, but everything had been carefully wiped clean. I think the shell was removed because it was easier to take it away altogether than to take it out and wipe it clean of prints.'

Hanson said, 'That makes sense. When you tried sitting at the study desk a few minutes ago, you were trying out a mental reconstruction. Damien Hardwick wasn't sitting at his desk when he was shot, yet he had been interrupted in the middle of a sentence in the letter he was writing.'

He paused thoughtfully, and his sergeant said, 'Go on.'

'Well, it suggests, obviously, that he was startled. Of all the people he would be *least* surprised to find in the house, his wife would be top of the list. Everyone moves differently. In a family, if you're in one room and you hear someone moving about in another room, you almost always know who it is, without looking, because everyone's habits are so familiar to you: this one lets the door bang, that one always speaks to the dog — you know what I'm saying?'

Thorpe nodded.

'We know from the medical evidence that Damien Hardwick was killed soon after lunch — soon after his wife left to go back to work. So if she'd come back, the natural thing would have been for him to assume she'd forgotten something. Even if he heard her open the cabinet where the gun was kept, there was nothing to alarm him because the cabinet also served as a bookcase. Yet he stopped writing in the middle of a sentence, got up and took several steps towards the door before he was shot. If Mrs Hardwick shot him, he should have been so unsuspecting he'd never even have turned his head. She could have shot him where he sat.'

Again the sergeant sat for a considerable number of seconds before saying, 'I know. But it's all pure conjecture. Something made him get up quickly, presumably to investigate a noise which was unexpected and unexplained. There's nothing conclusive about anything.'

He sighed, then smiled. 'Still, we may yet find that hypothetical small boy on a bicycle who saw something significant. We need him. Meanwhile, let's do some more knocking on doors and asking people to remember whether they saw or heard anything helpful.'

3

In the following string of days, filled with the hassles and sheer work of sorting, packing her belongings and looking for a house, Brooke saw nothing of the police, though her thoughts were endlessly dogged by wondering what they were doing, and when they would come back.

She found, to her delight, a recently renovated cottage for rent on a quiet side-road on the fringe of town. Members of Damien's congregation, evidently not yet sharing the police suspicions of her, had cheerfully helped her to move to the cottage, even providing a van and willing hands to shift furniture.

Church authorities had assured her there was no need to rush into vacating the vicarage, but on the last day, which she had spent cleaning the empty house, she walked slowly from room to room, remembering. Remembering the joy with which she had first come here as Damien's wife. Remembering her bewilderment at the first indications that the joy would be short-lived. Remembering the shock, anger and, in the end, unthinkably, fear.

She walked out, pulled the front door to, and drove away feeling oddly, for the first time since Damien's death, grief. Not truly grief at his death. She still felt guilty that she didn't feel grief over that. But she felt a strange, deep grief for the lost promise, for the man he almost was.

Now, she thought, somehow she had to get on with her life. There was no thought in her mind of leaving this little town in the hinterland of Queensland's Sunshine Coast. Although she had set up her landscaping business here only a year before she married Damien, she had a strong sense of belonging.

It was a town small enough for most people to know each other at least slightly, though that was becoming less true as more and more retirees found it to their liking, and their presence created employment, and so the town's population grew.

Broadfell was one of a series of townships and villages strung along the top of the broad-headed range which dropped down on the east to the towns and farmland — especially sugarcane — and tracts of bushland, the whole mix spreading out to the coast and the Pacific, fringed with pale, golden beaches and black rocks and ever-expanding coastal towns and resorts. To the west, the range fell away to farming valleys and forest and native bushland, with more blunt, low ranges beyond.

In spite of the steadily increasing population, little or nothing had damaged its beauty yet, at least in Brooke's eyes.

This, for her, was home, and here she would rebuild her life. If she was allowed to.

By day she could sometimes shut out the dread with work, but in the nights it came back unrelentingly: what if? What if she was arrested? She had no way of proving her innocence. It was no use to tell herself that neither could the police prove her guilt. What if they could make a strong enough case against her — not out of malice or inept handling of the investigation, but simply because so much pointed to her guilt. Motive. Opportunity. No alibi. What if that was enough to convince a jury? What if some well-meaning person had seen a car like hers near the vicarage that day, at a time when she claimed to be thirty kilometres away — and that person believed it was her car, and said so? What if . . .

She had to shut it out, cram her life so full of work that she had no time for other thoughts. Cram her life with so much work she would go home each night so exhausted that perhaps she could sleep.

With this in mind, she drove into the yard of Greenlands Landscaping just as Dean Pollock, her irrepressible young partner, was loading the Greenlands truck. Tall, lean, red-haired and twenty-four, Dean loved life, girls, and his work with equal zest.

When people had told her, in some alarm, that he was too irresponsible for the trust she was placing in him, she had nevertheless recognized his essential kindness and honesty as well as his artistic sense and his enthusiasm.

He greeted her now with a wide grin. 'Hi, Mrs H. — reporting for duty? I *need* you.'

She smiled. It was good to be back. 'You mean, I suppose, that you've plunged us into insolvency and total ruin?'

'Nope. Did my best to, but the wheels just kept rolling. I'm on my way to that new motel garden job. The groundwork's just about tidied up and we'll be ready to plant tomorrow. I don't suppose you could nip over to the nursery that thieving friend of yours runs, and pick up the plants I ordered? She promised she'd have them ready by this arvo. And don't forget to count 'em. Tell her I said so.'

'I'll go and get them. I'll need the trailer.'

'I'll hitch it on to this heap of tin of yours if you just back it over here.'

Brooke smiled with the amused lifting of spirits Dean's irreverent banter so often gave her. The thieving friend he referred to was Patricia Evans who, after her husband's death, had flung herself into carrying on the nursery business they had run together. Dean and Patricia were great friends, but he never allowed her to forget that once, when Greenlands had ordered and paid for fifty shrubs and trees, they had been delivered one shrub short.

Patricia greeted her friend with a pleased smile. 'Brooke! You're back at work.' She nodded at the trailer. 'Have you moved into the new house — actually moved?'

'Yes. I slept there last night and just went back to the other house this morning to give it a final clean now that my stuff is out. My slave-driving partner sent me over to collect the things he's ordered for the motel garden job.'

'Right. They're all ready.' Her eyes twinkled. 'I bet he told you to count them, too. I'll just ask Barnaby to load them into the trailer for you.' Barnaby Woods and his nineteen-year-old daughter, Jenny, worked for Patricia in the nursery.

'Cameron sprained his ankle when he fell out of a tree at a friend's place yesterday and the doctor ordered him to stay home from school for a couple of days to rest it,' Patricia went on. 'His new teacher dropped in over the lunch-break to see him. He's gone up to the house, so I'd better go too, and be a bit sociable, because it was kind of Mr Alford to come. Come along for a minute and say hello to Cameron. It'll cheer him up. It's nothing serious, but he's disgusted at himself because he'll miss soccer practice and at least one match. Even nine-year-olds take their sport seriously. Perhaps especially nine-year-olds.'

Guided by the sound of voices coming from the side veranda of the house, which backed on to the reasonably extensive grounds of the plant nursery, they found Cameron in a timber patio-chair, with his right foot on a stool and a golden Labrador dozing beside him, chatting comfortably with a tallish man with curling black hair.

'Hi, Brooke,' Cameron said cheerfully. Tall for his years, height and fair hair inherited from his father, blue eyes from his mother, he had an effervescence about him which stopped sufficiently short of cockiness to give him a quality which made him liked by both adults and his peers.

He made a wry face. 'As if it isn't enough that I'm wounded and suffering, Mr Alford brought around some *school-work* so I can keep in touch with what the others are doing. Isn't it the pits?'

'Absolutely,' Brooke agreed, 'but if you're so clumsy you can't climb a tree without falling out of it, it probably serves you right.'

'Falling!' He rolled his eyes in mock despair. 'Who fell? A branch broke, treacherous thing. I used to climb on it, but I've grown so much it couldn't take my hulking weight.'

'Weight?' Brooke said. 'Weight? You wouldn't weigh five stone wringing wet in an army overcoat. You fell, I'll bet.'

'Five stone,' he said sorrowfully. 'I never realized you were so old. We weigh people in kilograms in the real world.'

They all laughed, even Tom Alford clearly able to recognize the firm friendship behind the verbal banter.

Patricia made the introductions, and Tom Alford asked, 'Do you have children at the school, Mrs Hardwick?'

Brooke shook her head. 'No. No children.'

'But you live in Broadfell? Obviously you know this young villain quite well.'

'Yes. I'm in the landscaping business, which is how I met Patricia in the first place. I need her nursery.'

And I also badly need her friendship right now, she added mentally.

'Are you Greenlands Landscaping? I've seen the premises. Have you lived here long?'

'Four years. I drove through here once on a long weekend and I liked it so much I quit the job I had with a landscaping place in Brisbane, and set up here on my own. Then I took on a business partner, and married the local Anglican minister.'

She saw comprehension turn his face grave, his intense brown eyes understanding.

'I'm so sorry. I've been blundering on. Your name didn't immediately register.'

She smiled. 'There's no reason it should have, especially as you haven't lived here long.'

He nodded. 'Which reminds me I'd better get back to the school or I may not have a job here.' He smiled at Patricia, ruffled Cameron's hair and said, 'Take care of that ankle. We all miss you at school. It's so peaceful it doesn't seem normal.'

Cameron grinned. 'Sorry about that, sir. Thanks.'

'Thank you for coming, Mr Alford,' Patricia said. 'It was very kind of you.'

'My pleasure.' He turned and walked away, and something in the simple movement jolted Brooke's memory.

She had met Thomas Alford before. In the shadows behind the church when she had expected to pour out her pent-up misery to her cousin Harley, and had instead flung herself into a stranger's arms. Arms, she recalled with a clarity which surprised her, which had given comfort without hesitation or question, without even the smallest strings attached.

At least, she thought thankfully as she and Patricia walked back to the nursery, Tom Alford could have no way of knowing who she was, so she was still spared that embarrassment.

If she looked as stunned as she felt, Patricia didn't seem to notice, but said quietly, 'Brooke, have you heard anything more from the police?'

'No. I've seen them around the town, no doubt asking questions.' She smiled wryly. 'Looking for that small boy on his bicycle, or his equivalent. Have they talked to you?'

Patricia nodded. 'And to Maree. Not expecting us to have witnessed anything, of course, though they did ask Maree if she'd noticed any strangers in town that day. She asked them if they were joking, and explained, of course, that at least half the people who go into the coffee shop are strangers passing through.' She hesitated. 'Mostly they asked about your relationship with Damien.'

64

'They would, naturally. And?'

'We both said you'd never mentioned problems.' She stopped and looked at Brooke, her face troubled. 'It's getting to you, isn't it? The suspicion, the not knowing. How can they think you might have killed him? How can they?'

Brooke smiled a grim smile which didn't reach her eyes. The lines of strain were showing around her mouth and in the unconscious tenseness of her shoulders, and there were shadows under her eyes. 'Why wouldn't they?' she said bitterly. 'I can't prove I didn't. *Someone* did. Someone who knew him, who knew that house, very well. Why not me? Damien wrote all that stuff in his diary about my supposed strange behaviour — irrational mood-swings and so on. He couldn't have made a better job of pointing suspicion at me if he'd tried.'

'Are you sure he wasn't unbalanced? To the level where he thought what he was writing was true?'

'I'm sure he was unbalanced to some degree, but not to the point where he imagined things like that. He wrote those diary entries for a purpose, but what that purpose was, I don't know.'

She sighed wearily. 'I lived with him for three years, and I'm beginning to think I didn't know the first thing about him. I'm not sure of anything any more.'

Then she forced a quick smile. 'I believe the police will eventually find out who killed Damien. I have to believe that. I just hope it's soon. Now I must thank Barnaby for loading the plants into the trailer for me, and then get them over to the motel site ready for planting tomorrow.'

★ ★ ★

Detective Sergeant Harold Thorpe stopped beside the desk where Detective Hanson was frowning over a file, and dropped a diary on the desk top.

'Evidently you're not just a pretty face after all,' he said.

'The late Reverend Damien Hardwick's diary. You were right, according to the experts. There is reason to suspect very strongly that those entries concerning Mrs Hardwick's erratic behaviour and possible drug use were fictitious. Inspector Stone was sufficiently curious to get a police psychiatrist to read them, and on his advice they were sent to the forensic mob.'

David Hanson picked up the diary and looked up at his sergeant. 'Really? And?'

'All the entries in the diary, in forensic's

opinion, were written at the same time. Don't ask me how they reached that conclusion, but the handwriting experts had something to do with it — there's pages of details on their findings.'

He shrugged. 'Just how conclusive it is, I couldn't say. The psychiatrist found several errors in dates when Hardwick wrote things had happened. He — the shrink — gives it as his opinion that Hardwick always intended the diary to be made public. He wanted to point a finger at his wife for some reason. The learned doctor says it could — and he emphasizes could — indicate an intention on the part of the writer to murder his wife, possibly by means of a drug overdose, and make it appear suicide.'

'My God,' Hanson said softly. 'But why on earth would he want to murder her? I mean, if he fancied the bishop's daughter or the barmaid at the Rose and Crown, there's always divorce — easy enough these days. Twelve months' separation and you've an out. And money would hardly be the motive. I don't imagine there's any fortune involved.'

'There isn't. The inspector checked.' The sergeant perched on the edge of the desk. 'As you say, if one spouse wants to be free of the other, divorce is the logical option. But as we both know, it's not, sadly, the only option taken. And it may not look so good in an Anglican minister, especially one who valued his public face, or was particularly ambitious.'

'But — dammit, Sarge! A *minister* — to kill his own wife?'

'Ah! But don't forget his wife told us, in what appeared to be total sincerity, that the charming young clergyman was not quite what he seemed. I recall you were moved to quote Shakespeare.'

'Something rotten in the State of Denmark? Seems she was right.'

'Yes. But it still doesn't mean she didn't kill him. On the contrary. She told us she was afraid of his threat to frame her over drugs. If that was true, she had a reason to decide to strike first.'

Detective Hanson turned the diary over restlessly in his hands. 'So you said once before, and, yes, I agree she had possible motive. Probably opportunity. Doesn't mean we've got much against her, does it?'

'No. And it also leaves us with absolutely nothing against anyone else.'

They were silent for a few moments. Then the detective said thoughtfully, 'Sarge, do you know anything about that oddball religious group that have that sort of commune down off the range, back of Benton's Reach somewhere? Hardwick had some of their literature in his desk. It just struck me as a bit odd at the time.'

The sergeant grinned. 'You think the good vicar may have been about to disclose some villainous goings-on and they sent a hit-man to silence him?'

Hanson shrugged. 'Religion can be trumped-up as a cover sometimes. Usually for conning people so some smart guy makes money.'

'Not there, I suspect. I've been out there, actually. You're not the only one with a nasty, suspicious mind. I was willing to bet they had a nice little marijuana crop out there, or an amphetamine factory, so I paid a friendly visit, all unofficial, just an interested guy wanting to check out their recipe for peace. Not a copper at all. I didn't fool them for a minute, but they were mildly amused, not upset. As far as I could tell, and from what I've heard, they're entirely on the level. There's no restraint on comings and goings, family visits, or whatever. They're mostly people who have turned away from mainstream living, though some have ordinary jobs outside the community. They live simply but comfortably. Their main restriction seems to be that they're totally drug, tobacco and alcohol free.'

He pursed his lips. 'One bloke didn't seem

too pleased to see me, I felt, though I'm not sure why I thought so.'

'Copper's instinct born of long disillusionment with the human race?'

'Something like that. As for the literature Hardwick had, I should imagine lots of clergymen are interested to look at someone else's ideas about religion and the best way to live your life. But I think you can forget looking for the vicar's killer among that lot.'

4

The days ran into weeks and the newspapers had long since stopped speculating about the murder of an Anglican minister in his own vicarage; and though Brooke never doubted for a moment that the police believed she was the killer, and worked quietly and patiently to prove it, she rarely saw them.

Other people, she assumed, did see the police — no doubt were questioned by them. She could imagine the line the questioning would take: You work near the vicarage where the fatal incident occurred; do you recollect seeing or hearing anything unusual that afternoon? Did you see Mrs Hardwick leave for work? Or return? Would you recognize her car if you saw it parked in a side-street? You knew the Hardwicks; how would you rate their marriage? Have you heard rumours that Mrs Hardwick used hard drugs?

On nights when sleep refused to come no matter how tired she was, the imagined questions would repeat themselves through her brain. Damningly, people would certainly have heard rumours that she used illegal drugs, because Damien himself had launched the rumour. And no one would have any doubt, any hesitation in saying that his reaction may well have been anger; it was likely there would have been arguments — bitter arguments.

And so the case against her would build, or did so endlessly in her mind.

The new minister, the Reverend Hamish Black, was a pleasant, middle-aged man with twinkling eyes and a plump, happy-go-lucky wife. Brooke had kept up her involvement with the mid-week games group, the Wednesday club, and with the choir. Hamish and Rosemary Black had warmly approved both ventures.

Brooke saw nothing odd in a phonecall she received from Rosemary, who said several members of the Wednesday club had urged her — Rosemary — to take over the running of it, in order to let Brooke have more time to herself to get her life back together again in peace.

'People really seem to feel it would be best for you,' Rosemary Black had said, sounding uncomfortable, as if she had been asked to do something she would have preferred to avoid.

'Well,' Brooke said, 'I guess a break wouldn't be a bad idea. I do get rather weary. Thanks, Rosemary.'

It wasn't until several days later that

Brooke realized there may have been something more than concern for her welfare behind that phonecall.

There was a phonecall from the retired music teacher Brooke had persuaded to become conductor of the church choir, which had now expanded into singing much more than purely church music. A tall, thin man with grey hair and a passionate love of music which was infectious, he spoke to Brooke with a crisp formality quite unlike his usual cheerful manner.

'Mrs Hardwick, I feel it's time you took a break from the choir. You look very tired and tense, and choir-practice makes demands on you which you can well do without right now. You got the choir up and running. You still do most of the organizing. You've done your share. Now take a break.'

'But I enjoy it!' Brooke protested in astonishment. 'The singing and everything connected with choir is good therapy for me. It's not stressful. It's relaxing. I truly enjoy it.'

'No,' the conductor said firmly. 'It's time you took a break. I insist. Later on, of course. But not now.'

He hung up.

Brooke understood then, quite clearly. She was a murder-suspect, and people preferred not to be associated with her. And it was no 'ordinary' murder, if there ever could be such a thing. This was the murder of their loved minister. It had touched the whole village in a very personal way.

Many people treated her exactly as they always had. But she could never forget that the shadow of suspicion was always at her shoulder. In a bid to push it as far into the background as possible, she immersed herself in her work to a level where both Maree and Patricia urged her not to drive herself so hard, and even Dean Pollock asked if she was trying to make him redundant.

'Ease up,' he told her, serious for once. 'You're pushing yourself too hard, Brooke. At the rate you're going, you're heading straight for a breakdown.'

She smiled, touched by his concern. He, for one, certainly showed no signs of harbouring dark suspicions of her.

'If I'm tired enough,' she told him, 'there's always the chance I'll sleep.'

He frowned. 'Are you afraid? I mean, afraid of intruders? You shouldn't be living alone, if that's it.'

'No, Dean, I'm not afraid of intruders.'

My fear is a different kind of fear, she thought bitterly; the chill fear I live with is the fear that one day the police will feel they have enough evidence to arrest me. And I have not one shred of evidence in my defence.

It wasn't the slightest use to tell herself that it wouldn't happen. It only needed one genuinely mistaken individual to believe they'd seen her or her car near the vicarage at the appropriate time on the fatal day. Something as simple as an honest mistake could be, for the police — and, perhaps, in time, for a jury — enough to be convinced of her guilt.

She was in the office shortly after three one sunny afternoon when Tom Alford came in with an apologetic smile.

'I'm disturbing you. I should have phoned.'

She returned his smile. 'I love to be disturbed when I'm doing the accounts. Not my favourite part of the job. How can I help you?'

'Well, the thing is, I've bought a house which is just newly built. It seems the owners were city people who intended to retire here, but the husband died suddenly and the wife no longer wants to come, and so the place was put up for sale. I like the house, but of course the yard is just raw earth, and I haven't the creative imagination to design a garden, and I do want a garden. So I wondered if your landscaping business would take on the job — at least of the design.'

'Yes, of course. Where is the house?'

'On Apple-tree Crescent.'

'Oh, yes,' she nodded. 'I've seen that house while it was under construction. It has a lovely outlook, right out to the coast. The block slopes away a bit in one corner, doesn't it? I remember thinking briefly that it would be an interesting block to set a garden on. I think we'd enjoy doing that. If you bring in a site-plan I could have a think about it and perhaps come out at the weekend, when you're free to be there. I'd like Dean, my partner, to have a look also.'

'Well,' he said hesitantly, 'I did bring a plan of the site with me.' He glanced at his watch. 'Can you leave this place unattended for fifteen minutes and come and have a cup of coffee with me while we look at the plan?'

She looked up to say no, and remembered she hadn't bothered with lunch. She smiled. 'Thank you. I'll just put the answering machine on to tell callers to dial my mobile phone if they really want me urgently.'

At 'Maree's' she introduced Maree and Tom Alford, and Maree said, 'Oh, you're the new teacher young Cameron Evans told me about. And Brooke, that six-foot streak of pump-water, your cousin Harley, is in town.' She looked up. 'And speaking of the devil . . .'

'Hi, Brooke,' his familiar, lazy voice said from behind her.

'Hal!' She jumped up and kissed his cheek in delight. 'What are you doing here on a working day?' Then, anxiously, 'There's nothing wrong, is there?'

He grinned. 'Not unless you count the fact that I'm about to become a permanent resident of Broadfell. Do you remember, the night of the funeral, that Maree mentioned the local pharmacy was up for sale? Well, I didn't want to tell you until the deed was done, but I came to see it, liked what I saw, have been negotiating, and lo! it is mine, as of half an hour ago.'

'But that's grand! Maree, you look like the cat that stole the cream. You've known this was going on?'

She smiled. 'Well, yes. But I was sworn to secrecy, in case it all fell through. Harley didn't want you disappointed. Now, what can I get you and Mr Alford?'

'Oh, I'm so sorry. I'm being terribly rude,' Brooke said swiftly, and made the introduction of the two men.

Tom Alford shook hands with Harley and said quietly to Brooke, 'I'll leave you to chat with your cousin. It seems you've a lot to talk about. I'll make an appointment to have you or your partner have a look at the plans at a more convenient time.'

Before Brooke could protest, he picked up the not yet unrolled site-plan and walked out.

Maree said, 'He actually looked a bit miffed, Brooke. You could still have discussed whatever the work was, couldn't you? I mean, it wasn't anything terribly confidential, or controversial, was it?'

Brooke shook her head. 'No. Just a house-block.'

But she suddenly knew why Tom Alford had looked slightly stunned. She had called Harley by his childhood nickname, just as she had on the night she mistook Tom Alford for him, and had flung herself into a stranger's arms.

The vicar's widow in a lovers' tryst, the night of her husband's funeral.

That was how Tom Alford would see it. She had a moment's desire to rush after him and explain, but Harley was pulling out a chair and asking what she'd have to eat, and anyway, why should she care what Tom Alford thought?

★ ★ ★

But she found she did care, and after she had finished work at the Greenlands office that evening, she drove around to his house, wondering whether in fact he and his family had moved in. There were lights on, and he answered the doorbell with a surprised lift of one eyebrow.

'Mrs Hardwick! It's very kind of you, but there was no need to put yourself to any trouble. There's not all that much urgency about my landscaping plans.'

Brooke shook her head. 'That's not why I'm here. I feel I owe you an explanation.' She hesitated. 'No, that's not quite true. I think I owe it to *myself* to give you an explanation. You know that we've met — even before we met at Patricia Evans's nursery that day.'

'Mrs Hardwick,' he said flatly, 'I'm not about to spread gossip about you, or to judge you. It's none of my business.'

'No,' she said impatiently, 'that's not why I'm here. I suppose I shouldn't care in the least what you think. But I would still like to tell you what that meeting behind the church was about.'

He studied her for a few seconds in the light from the front door. Then he shrugged and stepped back. 'You'd better come in.'

'Won't I be disturbing your wife? She's probably preparing dinner.'

'I have no wife and I hadn't yet begun to fix a meal, so you're disturbing no one.'

He led the way through to a spacious

living-room, tastefully and simply furnished — pale walls and floor and warmly dark furniture with bright cushions, and wide windows that looked across the eastern veranda and away to the distant string of lights along the coast.

Brooke exclaimed with involuntary delight, 'What a lovely outlook! I hadn't quite realized what the night view would be.'

'Yes, I was fortunate the place was on the market, even though it's surrounded by bare earth at the moment.'

He waved her to a comfortable chair and sat facing her. 'May I ask how long you've known I was the man behind the church?'

'Since I met you at Patricia's the day you called to see how Cameron's sprained ankle was. I hoped you'd never know who that somewhat distraught woman at the church was, but of course I gave myself away this afternoon when I called my cousin Harley by the nickname he had when we were children: Hal.'

She paused. 'We grew up in the same neighbourhood. We were both without brothers or sisters of our own, so we became like brother and sister to each other. We've always been very close, but never romantically involved. When I moved here, we didn't often see each other, especially after I married

Damien. My marriage wasn't a happy one. More recently it was very unhappy indeed, but neither Damien nor I allowed it to become obvious. He was very popular with his parishioners, and quite frankly he deserved to be, because if I could put it in an odd sort of way, he was very good at his job.'

She smiled ruefully. 'I kept up appearances for the sake of my own pride, probably, rather than for Damien's sake. I didn't even confide in Maree or Patricia, my closest friends, while Damien was alive. But sometimes I felt I had to tell someone just a little. Harley was the one I could talk to — and let off some emotional steam. The day of the funeral, I asked him to stay and meet me in private. I needed, desperately, some kind of comfort that was not comfort for grief. There was any amount of that sort of sympathy being offered to me by kind and sincere people. But there was no one I could turn to who understood that I didn't — couldn't — feel grief. I was ashamed I couldn't. I was shocked, appalled, yes — but not grief-stricken. I asked Harley to meet me in secret because no one would understand it was innocent. There were likely to be kind and concerned people at the house. But I desperately needed . . . '

She stopped and looked down at her hands, clasped in her lap. 'It must sound totally crazy to you, but I needed exactly the sort of unquestioning comfort you gave me.'

She stood up. 'I'm sorry to sound an utter fool. You must find all this as embarrassing as I do. I just wanted you to *know*, that's all.' She smiled. 'Thank you for listening. And thank you for being so kind, that night. You can never know how much you helped me.'

She turned quickly and walked out and drove away.

Her rented cottage was naturally in darkness as she put the car in the garage. Mostly in winter she arrived home from work in the dark, but now that spring had come the days were lengthening and soon the long, hot summer days would mean she would be home with enough daylight left to do some work in her own garden in the cool of the evenings.

On the drive home she had wondered over and over just what Tom Alford would make of her visit. He very well might conclude that only a guilty conscience, not a clear one, would drive her into making an explanation of sorts for arranging a secret meeting with Harley Wilson. Well, what he thought didn't matter now. She had told him the truth, and if he chose not to believe her, that was his right.

It would be good to have Harley living in

Broadfell. She smiled a little and wondered how much of his decision to move was due to the instant rapport he had struck with Maree. Looking back, she recalled how they had got along very comfortably from the moment they'd met, that evening of the funeral. Obviously he had kept Maree informed of his intention to buy the local pharmacy. In spite of running a very successful business in her coffee shop, Maree was not a person who made close friends easily, but the easygoing Harley clearly had a special relationship with her which was rather more than only friendship.

Feeling pleased for both of them, Brooke fitted her key into the lock and thought, I'll get a dog or a kitten; maybe both. Damien wouldn't have animals but I'd love one or two. Nothing fancy — just a waif wanting a home.

With a lift of her spirits at the thought, she opened the front door and stepped inside, flicking on the living-room light.

An arm went hard around her waist and a hand was clamped over her mouth before her shocked brain had more than a second to register the sight of a man sitting in her favourite easy chair.

A man neatly dressed in a grey suit and blue shirt and a striped tie. Perfectly ordinary and unremarkable, except that he wore gloves and had a black balaclava pulled over his head, and held a kitchen-knife with a six-inch blade.

The man behind her, who held her in a savagely hard grip, also wore gloves. She could feel the fabric of a glove — leather, some part of her brain noted — against the skin of her face. She also noted, with a strange detachment born no doubt of shock, that there had been no attempt to trash the room. Nothing appeared to have been disturbed.

That, she recalled chillingly, had also been true of the vicarage the night Damien was murdered.

The man in the chair stood up and took a step towards her. She looked down at the knife in his hand, and the same curiously detached part of her brain which had registered the undisturbed room noted that the knife was almost certainly from her own kitchen. They killed Damien with his own shotgun, she thought numbly; now they're going to kill me with my own kitchen-knife. I wonder if they'll tell me why.

'Good-evening, Mrs Hardwick,' the man with the knife said. His voice was quite pleasant; his manner, strangely, seemed uncontrivedly courteous. 'We need your co-operation, so if you promise not to scream or do anything foolish, my friend will let you go. Do you promise?'

She nodded, and the man behind her took his hand from around her mouth and, taking her arm, propelled her to a chair facing the man with the knife.

'Sit down,' he said, and when she obeyed he released her arm and stepped around to stand beside his companion. He was taller and less stocky, but also neatly dressed in a blue shirt, navy suit, patterned tie, plus the anonymity of a black balaclava.

The man with the knife stepped closer. 'Where's the stuff, Mrs Hardwick?'

Bewilderment momentarily pushed fear fractionally aside, and she said, 'Pardon?'

'Where's the stuff?'

She shook her head. 'I don't know what you mean.'

'Don't play games with us. We need the stuff your husband had.' The voice was hard, now, the courtesy gone.

'What stuff? What are you talking about? Do you mean drugs?'

The second man said contemptuously, 'You know very well we're talking about — '

'Wait!' the man with the knife interrupted. 'What if she doesn't know?'

'She must know, all right.'

'Maybe. But if she doesn't, we don't want to spread the word, do we?'

'But she must know.'

Brooke said desperately, 'I don't have the faintest idea what it is that you want, but whatever it is, if it belonged to my husband, it would have been in the other house, not here. He never lived here.'

'We know that.' The man with the knife was impatient now. More than impatient, Brooke thought: he was intensely anxious. 'Of course it isn't here, nor at the vicarage, either. He would never have kept it there. So where would he keep it?'

'I don't know!' There was an edge of desperation in her voice. 'How can I know where he'd keep a thing if I don't know what it is?'

'Then start thinking. He'd know lots of people. Think. Who would he know who'd store something for him and not ask questions? Never be suspicious? Someone, maybe, without a family — well, no children. Children poke around a lot.'

Brooke shook her head. The numbness of shock was still dulling the edge of fear, but she could scarcely drag her eyes away from the knife in the hand of the man who was doing the talking. They will kill me, she thought. They killed Damien, I suppose, because he wouldn't tell them where the stuff was; now they'll kill me, because I *can't* tell them.

'Well?' the man with the knife snapped.

'I don't know. I suppose any number of people would hide something for him. Most people would trust him.'

'She knows,' the second man said coldly. 'Why else would she have killed him?'

'*What?*' Brooke felt fresh shock like a physical blow. 'What did you say?'

'Oh, come on,' the second man said harshly. Here there was no courtesy, nor pretence of it. 'Don't play cute bloody games. Everyone with a brain in their head must know you killed him. Who else had a reason? You knew he had the stuff, and you got all conscientious about it, and you reckoned if you killed him you'd put a stop to it. So where is it?'

He stepped forward and hit her across the face with his open hand — not a vicious blow, but stingingly a reminder of her helplessness.

'No more of that,' the man with the knife said to his companion. 'It's a waste of time on someone like her. I'd say she's the type you could beat to a pulp and she'd never tell you.'

Anger flickered for the first time through the fear and shock. 'You're right,' Brooke said bitterly. 'I'd never tell you because I don't *know*. And I did not kill my husband.'

'Really. Well, you wouldn't like anything nasty to happen to your sister, would you?'

She stared. The man had blue eyes, that detached part of her mind noted; though it was hard to tell, when you could see his eyes only through the holes of the balaclava. 'I don't have a sister.'

'No? Then who's that blonde lady who runs the coffee shop?'

She would have thought it wasn't possible to feel any more afraid, but this was different. Fear for someone else, she discovered, was in another dimension.

'Well? Isn't she your sister?' The rough, impatient voice.

'No.' Her throat felt too dry to even allow that one word, and it came out as a hoarse croak.

'You're lying. You're not very good at it. We'll be back. And by then you'd better have done some thinking. We want that stuff, understand?'

The man with the knife tossed it on to the floor, and they turned to walk out. Suddenly, for no particular reason that she could think of later, it seemed fearfully important to get the knife. She had not even the faintest thought of using it, but there was some vague feeling that if she had possession of it they

88

couldn't use it, either. It was a feeling born of the fact that she had believed from the moment she walked in the door that they would kill her.

She stood up to step toward the knife, and the man who had hit her before wheeled around and slammed his fist hard into her stomach.

As she doubled up in pain, struggling for the breath he had driven out of her body, he said, 'Had some thoughts of following to check number plates or something? Uh-uh. I don't think that would be a good idea.'

Then they were gone, and she slid to the floor on her knees, fighting to breathe against waves of pain and nausea. Gradually they subsided and she got unsteadily to her feet and stumbled to the phone. The police-officer who took the call seemed fairly uninterested when she told him the intruders had left, they had not stolen anything, and she had suffered only a minor assault. But he promised solemnly, 'Someone will be with you shortly, and meanwhile make sure the doors are locked, though it's most unlikely they'll be back.'

Brooke hung up, thinking, lock the doors; but the doors *were* locked — so how did they get in? She went through the cottage to the back door. It was closed, but not locked, although she had a clear recollection of having locked it before she went to work. It was a simple key-in-knob lock which, she had heard, was easily picked by anyone with know-how. She relocked it and pushed a kitchen chair with the back wedged under the door-knob. Her stomach was hurting and she was shivering from head to foot.

She thought about a cup of tea. Something hot might relax the bruised muscles. But she had to phone Maree first.

The front doorbell rang, and for a moment she simply froze, unable to move or think. Then she went slowly through the house to the door, thinking, they won't have come back; it isn't them. She wasn't convinced.

'Who is it?' she asked through the closed door.

'It's Tom Alford, Mrs Hardwick.'

'Tom.' It came out as a half-sob as she fumbled with the door latch, hands still shaking.

She opened the door and he said, 'Look, I've come to apologize for seeming like . . .' He stopped.

'You're ill!' he said sharply. 'Here, let me help you.' He caught her arm and guided her to the same chair she had sat in a few minutes before, facing two shapeless, balaclava-sculptured faces. 'I'll call a doctor.'

'No!' It was still difficult to get words out. 'It — I'm all right. There were two men.' She shuddered. 'I've called the police, but it's no use. They're gone and I've no idea who they were.'

He squatted on his heels in front of her and took one of her hands in both of his. 'What did they do to you?'

She shook her head. 'Nothing much. One punched me in the stomach when he thought I was going to follow them. But I didn't even think of doing that. I wanted to get the knife.'

'Knife!' He sounded shocked.

'That knife.' She pointed to where it still lay on the carpet. 'They were waiting, you see. Just waiting for me when I came home. In the house. One had the knife. It's one of my kitchen-knives.'

'What have they taken?' He looked quickly around the room.

'Nothing, as far as I know.' She was gaining control of her voice now, and beginning to think coherently. 'They wanted me to tell them where something was — something my husband was supposed to have had — drugs, apparently. You see,' she told him quietly, 'my husband had spread some rumours that I was using drugs. I never have, but I suppose they'd heard the rumours and got them confused and thought it was Damien who

91

had drugs. They thought I was lying, and they threatened . . . ' She leapt up. 'Dear, heaven, I must warn Maree.'

'Your friend who keeps the coffee shop? Why do you have to warn her?'

'They said I'd better try to think where Damien might have hidden what they kept calling 'the stuff', or something nasty might happen to Maree.' She was punching in the number on the phone as she spoke. 'They thought she was my sister.'

She waited. 'She's not answering.' There was fear in her voice.

'The shop will be closed, won't it?'

'Yes. It closes at five-thirty. But she should be at home, and she lives alone. That was her home number I called.'

'Tell me where she lives and I'll go and make sure she's all right.'

'Would you? She lives — Oh. I forgot. She's gone out to dinner with my cousin Harley. It was to be a celebration of the fact he's just bought the local pharmacy.'

She sat down and put her hands over her face. 'I'm babbling on and not making any sense to you, I'm afraid. I'm sorry. None of it makes any sense to me, either.'

'You've had a hell of a shock. I'll make some coffee. Or have you something stronger? Brandy?'

'There's brandy in that cabinet.'

She took the glass he handed her and sipped gratefully, closing her eyes for a minute as the spirit warmed and steadied her. Then she smiled wryly up at him.

'You seem to make a habit of being there when I desperately need someone.'

'It makes me feel useful,' he said lightly, a smile crinkling around the corners of his brown eyes. 'Now I think you'd better have some food. I'm a dab hand at scrambled eggs on toast. Sit and relax while I raid your kitchen. How long before the boys in blue get here?'

'I shouldn't think they'll be long. There's only one constable stationed here, and he could be away somewhere, and since I wasn't under immediate threat the officer who answered the call at the central office wouldn't feel it was urgent. But, truly, you've been more than kind already. You don't have to make dinner for me as well.'

'Well, I'm not leaving until the police come, and I haven't eaten yet, either, and I'm starving, so I'll be making dinner for two.' He grinned. 'But if it makes you feel better you can come and tell me where things are in your kitchen.'

He looked down at the knife on the carpet. 'Fingerprints?'

She shook her head. 'They wore gloves. And balaclavas.'

'Ah. Well, better leave it where it is, anyway, I suppose.'

She said slowly, 'I thought they must have been the ones who killed Damien. But they thought *I* had.'

He stared. 'You?'

She nodded. 'The police think so, too. My guess is they won't even believe there *were* any intruders tonight. They'll think I made it up.'

'But . . . '

As if on cue, the doorbell rang. To Brooke's surprise it was not uniformed men, but the two detectives.

'We were in the area,' Sergeant Thorpe told her as they seated themselves after being introduced to Tom Alford, 'so we thought we'd take the call.'

'Shall I go?' Tom asked quietly.

Brooke shook her head. 'No. Stay, please.'

They let her tell her story without interruption, and she told it carefully, trying to recall everything exactly as it happened. Detective Hanson made notes, the sergeant sat immobile, watching her.

'How much description can you give, Mrs Hardwick?' he asked expressionlessly when she had finished.

'The man with the knife was of medium height, stocky and spoke like a well-educated man. The other man — the one who hit me — was tall and thinner, and spoke more roughly, but not in an uneducated way. They both wore suits and ties and looked like businessmen. Except for the balaclavas. They were quite unremarkable, I suppose would be the best word.'

They asked a few more questions: had she noticed any vehicle parked in the street? Two or three, but there usually were and she had not taken any particular notice, and of course it was dark. Had she heard a vehicle start up after they left? No, but she'd been trying to get back some of the breath the punch had knocked out of her lungs. Ah, yes, very unpleasant, and what about Mr Alford: had he met a vehicle or seen two men walking away? No. And how had Mrs Hardwick seemed when he arrived? Extremely distressed and in some pain. And how long have you known Mrs Hardwick? Only met her once before today, wanted her to organize some landscaping.

'I see,' Sergeant Thorpe said. 'Well, we'll ask neighbours if they saw anything. Of course you haven't any really close neighbours here, and there are trees beside the house, but someone may have seen something useful.'

'What about Maree — Miss Stewart? They made a threat.'

'Almost certainly bluff. But we'll speak to Miss Stewart, and keep an eye on things.'

Detective Hanson looked keenly at Brooke. 'Are you sure you don't need a doctor?'

She shook her head. 'I was shocked and I was terrified. But I'm not injured. I was winded and I dare say I'll have some sore abdominal muscles for a day or two, but that's all.'

She shivered. 'Except that I'm very concerned for Maree Stewart.'

She gripped her hands together in her lap and looked at the spot on the floor where the balaclava-masked intruder had tossed the knife.

'It's a very effective form of extortion, isn't it? To threaten to harm someone you care about if you don't co-operate,' she said bleakly.

'It's also particularly cowardly,' the sergeant said with a suddenly surprising edge of quiet anger. 'Like all forms of extortion.'

Brooke looked up at him. 'Well, I think it would have worked in my case, if I'd had anything to tell them. But I haven't. I don't know whether my husband had access to any drugs. If he did, it wouldn't be for personal use — only to put him in a position to make good the threat he held over me.'

After a moment she added bleakly, 'And if he had some, and gave them in some innocent-looking package to an unsuspecting someone to keep for him, that someone could be absolutely anyone.'

Sergeant Thorpe nodded. 'Nevertheless, we'll make inquiries.'

'Mrs Hardwick,' Detective Hanson said suddenly, 'are you certain you don't know either of those men? I know you couldn't see their faces. But obviously *they* knew *you*. Not only had they apparently heard rumours that there were drugs in the picture, they knew you and Miss Stewart are close friends. At the very least, they have been watching you. Think: voices, mannerisms.'

Brooke nodded understanding, and was silent, closing her eyes to rerun the scene in her mind. No one spoke. Then she opened her eyes and shook her head.

'I'm certain they're not men I know well. One — the one with the knife — I think I may have heard his voice somewhere. But it's not a voice I know well, and it may be just a voice which reminds me of another. There's nothing else remotely familiar about either of them. That's not to say I haven't seen them somewhere, sometime, or they have seen me.'

'If you heard that man's voice again, you'd remember it?'

'I think so, yes.' She gave a little shiver. 'I hope I never do hear it.'

'Mmm,' the sergeant said. 'Meanwhile, why not go to stay with Miss Stewart, or, better, ask her to come to stay with you — just as a precaution, and more for reassurance for both of you. It's unlikely these men will resort to violence against either of you, but we can't be certain.'

He stood up with his customary economy of movement, and the two detectives said good-night and left, with assurances that a patrol car would keep an eye on her cottage and Maree's flat. In view of the scarcity of police and patrol cars in the area, Brooke felt it was a rather empty assurance.

She locked the door behind them and went slowly back into the sitting-room, and stopped abruptly. Tom Alford wasn't there.

'Tom!' she said sharply on a note of near-alarm.

'In the kitchen, fixing those scrambled eggs,' he answered cheerfully. 'Sit down and I'll bring the food in.'

She found she was surprisingly glad to sit down and do nothing except wonder what time Maree would be home from dinner with

Harley. Tom Alford brought in two steaming plates of eggs on toast, and when they had eaten he fetched two mugs of coffee.

'Where did your friend Maree and your cousin go for dinner? You might contact them at the restaurant.'

'I don't know. Almost certainly to a restaurant up here on the range somewhere, because there are some excellent ones, and they wouldn't want to be too late home, because Harley only just today tied up the purchase of the local pharmacy, so he still has to go back to Brisbane tonight. He hasn't wound up his business there.'

'Does Maree have an answering machine?'

'She does, yes. But she mightn't check for messages when she comes in.'

'Phone and leave a message for her to call you back tonight, urgently. I'll stay here till she phones, or if she doesn't within a reasonable time, I'll go around to her place and make sure she gets the message as soon as she gets home — or wake her if she's home already.'

'That sounds wonderful. Thank you. You're very kind.'

'I never got around to telling you why I came round tonight.' He smiled ruefully. 'My reaction in the coffee shop when I realized where we'd first met must have made me seem like some appalling stiff-necked prig. I was taken by surprise, of course, but I thought you hadn't realized who I was, and I just wanted to get out of there before you did realize it and become embarrassed by it. I was totally clumsy about it, of course. I'm sorry to have seemed to be behaving like a Victorian-era elderly maiden aunt.'

She shook her head. 'You'd every right to be taken aback. The vicar's widow in a clandestine meeting with another man on the night of her husband's funeral? It seems a distasteful betrayal at the very least.' She looked at him and said slowly, 'Can I ask you something I've no right to?'

'Fire away.'

'Why were you there, behind the church? Did I interrupt something?'

'Yes, as a matter of fact, you did,' he said solemnly.

'Oh, dear. Look, I'm sorry.'

He grinned with a glint of mischief. 'I'd heard that some of the fifth-graders liked to gather behind the church for a quiet smoke. I planned to give them a fright, but you'd probably already done it.'

In spite of the alarms of the evening she laughed. 'I had no idea there'd been so much pedestrian traffic behind the church that evening.'

Then she was serious and sipped the coffee gratefully for a moment, and then said quietly, 'It's grossly unfair to have burdened you with my troubles. I can't thank you enough for your kindness, but once I've contacted Maree you must just stop concerning yourself with me.'

He smiled. 'I don't think I'd find that very easy now. I don't like unfinished stories.'

'I'm serious, Tom. You're a teacher. Even in this day and age people expect teachers to set some sort of standard. It wouldn't do you any good to befriend a woman suspected of murdering her husband.'

'That's nonsense! No one's ever suggested such a thing to me, certainly. And no one with any intelligence would think it.'

Brooke smiled ruefully. 'Thank you for your trust, Tom. But no one with any intelligence could fail to at least consider the possibility. And you don't know me well enough to make a judgement. I assure you that whether or not anyone's spoken of it to you, even some of the people who know me reasonably well are beginning to have doubts. Though the police have been discreet, some of the questions they must be asking people must show what *they're* thinking. There's the rumour Damien started about me using drugs. It must have spread. Rumours do. It has to make people wonder.'

'But how do you know people suspect you?' He looked faintly scandalized. 'Surely no one's *said* so?'

'Oh, no, not in so many words. But people suddenly realize I must be too busy to work with the games group I organized for the young people. And they feel I must be still too distressed to practise with the choir. One couple who regularly invited Damien and me to dinner told me that they perfectly understood I wouldn't want to go on my own. What they meant was they didn't fancy risking arsenic in the coffee.'

The note of bitterness was clear enough in her voice.

'You see,' she went on quietly, 'the worst part is that even if the police never arrest me because they haven't enough evidence, unless they find the person who *did* kill Damien, I'll stand forever condemned in the eyes of some, and under suspicion in the eyes of the rest. I don't think the police have any doubt. Certainly my balaclava friends didn't.'

Tom was staring at her. 'I've never thought of it like that. I guess it's always like that for someone suspected of a crime they haven't committed, if the guilty party is never found. It's — quite awful. I'm sorry.'

He made an impatient gesture. 'What an

inanely inadequate thing to say.' He fell silent for a few moments, and then said hesitantly, 'Tell me it's none of my business and I'll accept that absolutely. But — you said to the police this evening that you didn't believe your husband would have had drugs in his possession unless it was so that he could make good his threat to you. Can you tell me what that was about?'

Brooke was cradling her empty coffee mug between her hands, looking beyond the comfortable little sitting-room, into a painful past. She nodded. 'I think I owe you that.'

She told him, briefly and unemotionally, not looking at the concern in his face.

'I can't explain what was wrong with Damien,' she finished. 'But something was. He wasn't normal. Not quite. It was almost as though he had — Oh, I don't know. I'm not qualified to make even a guess. But maybe it was some form of schizophrenia. At least you can't blame the police or anyone else for thinking I had a motive to kill him.'

They were both silent for a while, and then Brooke said, 'If you want to go home now, back to a sane and sensible life, and not speak to me again, I would agree that's what you should do.'

He didn't seem to have heard her. 'What

happened to your husband's belongings?' he asked.

Surprised, she echoed, 'Belongings?'

'Yes. Clothes, books, tools, suitcase, brief-case — anything and everything.'

'Well, I offered his mother all his personal things, like books, his watch and so on. She wouldn't have them, to my surprise. Whether it was because she never liked me and wouldn't take anything that looked like a gift from me, I don't know, but I guess so, whatever she said. Damien was an only child, so there wasn't anyone else. I — wanted nothing of his. His clothes went to the Salvation Army, his books to the local library, except his Bible and prayer-books, which I gave to some of his parishioners, likewise his watch. I have his music — tapes and CDs — and his letters and personal papers which I haven't sorted out for burning or putting in the garbage yet. Why do you ask?'

'I just thought that if he did have drugs, they would be hidden somewhere among his things.'

Brooke shook her head. 'The police thought of that. They searched. His things as well as mine.'

'Oh. Well, they'd certainly know more about doing a search than I would. I suppose there are common places where people hide things.'

'Like putting the front-door key under the mat to hide it from burglars?'

He grinned. 'That sort of thing. But I tell you what, school-children are pretty cunning at hiding things, too, and teachers learn some counter-cunning to outwit them.'

Brooke looked at him gravely. 'Are you talking abut drugs? With primary-school youngsters?'

Tom shrugged. 'It's a big, bad world out there — in places, anyway. Drugs aren't a big problem here, in Broadfell — not hard drugs. But there can be marijuana, even in the primary school, unfortunately. But of course, cigarettes are more common. All I'm saying is that there could be places the police didn't think of, that a teacher would think of straight off. But I sound as if I'm pushing my nose into your affairs. I didn't mean to. Sorry.'

'After all you've done for me I think you've every right to give me advice. You have some ideas, haven't you?'

'Only that when you mentioned that you have your husband's music, I just wondered. A music-cassette case can hold something other than a music tape. Maybe some time you might like to check. That's all.'

Brooke looked at him thoughtfully. 'There was something among Damien's papers that surprised me a little. I'd forgotten it. Oh, nothing like hidden drugs. Do you know anything about a religious group — at least I suppose you'd call them a religious group, though I'm not sure — called New Day?'

'New Day.' He shook his head. 'I can't recall hearing of it. Why?'

'They have some sort of commune down off the range near a district known as Bentons Reach. Damien seemed quite interested in them at one time, visited the place a couple of times at least, and then seemed to become disillusioned and said that only a couple of them were genuine. He didn't explain what he meant and I didn't ask. But when I gathered up his personal papers I noticed he had quite a lot of literature of theirs — pamphlets, even some correspondence. I didn't read any of it, but I still have it. It just at this moment occurred to me to wonder — I mean, while most minor religious groups are genuine, whether or not most of us regard them as way-out, there are a few which are very strange indeed, even a front for criminal activity.'

'You think your visitors may have come from there?'

Brooke sighed. 'I'm not sure what I think.

I've certainly no grounds for suggesting those men tonight may have come from there. I'm clutching at straws. I think the thing that suddenly came into the back of my mind was a fleeting thought that if that group was a front for something criminal, and Damien found out . . . '

'It could be possible they silenced him?'

Brooke shook her head. 'It doesn't make sense. Because it doesn't explain how they knew he had a shot-gun, let alone where he kept it.'

'Would you like to get that literature now and let's have a look at it?' Tom suggested. 'It would be one way to occupy our minds until your friend Maree gets home.'

Brooke fetched a large, brown envelope crammed with pamphlets and a couple of letters. There were about twenty identical pamphlets, consisting of a modest single-folded sheet of glossy paper with a couple of photographs, one of farmland and one of a cluster of small cottages. The printed matter explained that the New Day community, led by Brother George Macintosh, was a partially self-contained community of people, most of whom had suffered a variety of problems and traumas, particularly drug or alcohol related, and who chose to withdraw either totally or partially from mainstream society and seek

107

peace with God and their fellow-humans. They sought no outside financial support and rejected drugs, gambling and alcohol. Anyone who sincerely sought God's solace in simple living was welcome to visit and see for themselves whether this was the haven they wished.

A couple of Biblical quotes were strategically placed in the text, and it was all very pleasantly worded.

'They certainly don't sound likely to produce my visitors of tonight, nor any murderous home-invaders,' Brooke said.

'It looks as though your husband was going to distribute some of their pamphlets,' Tom said. 'Or they were hoping he would.'

Brooke unfolded one of the accompanying letters. 'Apparently he had already distributed some of the literature. This thanks him for his enthusiasm and is enclosing the extra pamphlets he requested.'

She pulled out two more letters. 'This one thanks him for visiting and displaying such interest in their humble work. The second one — this is dated only a couple of weeks before he was killed — this one says they would welcome him back at any time, and are sorry it's been a little while since they've seen him.'

She looked up at Tom. 'That must have

been written when he had lost interest in them. I wish now that I'd taken more notice of what he said about them.'

'Do you think,' Tom said slowly, 'that he really may have discovered that their idyllic retreat from the wicked world *was* in fact a front for something nasty?'

Brooke put the letters and pamphlets back into the bulky envelope. 'I don't know. I remember he seemed a bit angry — no, that's not quite right. He was more excited. Yes, I suppose it *was* rather as though he'd discovered something — something he proposed to take some action about. That's possibly what his mood was.'

'Then . . . ' Tom hesitated. 'If that was the case, and whatever he'd unearthed or suspected was big enough, they might even have chosen to silence him. Shouldn't you tell the police?'

Brooke shook her head. 'What do I have to tell them? Damien had been interested in the New Day group and then told me they weren't genuine. That's hardly an indication of criminal activity. And it wouldn't explain how someone from that group could have come, bent on murder, and just happened to unlock the hall cabinet to see if there was a weapon inside.'

'Ah. Yes, of course. I see the problem with

that theory. But even if the intruders tonight weren't the killers — and you say they genuinely seemed to believe *you* had killed your husband — suppose he'd confiscated something, most probably drugs, to use as evidence to expose some illegal activities of either the group or one or two individuals, and those thugs tonight came to take it back?'

'That wouldn't explain why they seemed sure I'd killed Damien because I had to stop him from doing something I found unconscionable.'

She sighed and put her head in her hands, and they both sat silently, thinking.

Eventually Brooke said, 'I think I'll take a drive down to New Day's little oasis and see whether I can get some sort of feel for what they're really about, whether or not they're all above board.'

'You mustn't!' he said sharply. 'If they're up to something illegal and it has *any* connection with Damien, they might take very strong exception to you going there.'

'Oh, I'd have a perfectly innocent reason for going. My husband had been very interested in their work. I just felt I'd like to see for myself.'

'You're not to go!' He stopped, and flushed. 'I'm sorry. I've no business lecturing you. But — well, if you insist on going, let me come with you.'

Brooke looked at him in surprise. 'That's very kind of you, but I couldn't presume any further on your kindness.' She smiled. 'You've already helped me greatly, twice.'

'It's not just kindness. I have to admit this New Day lot have aroused my curiosity, too. I'd like to go with you. I told you before that I don't like unfinished stories.'

'Then, thank you. I admit I'd be glad of company. Not that I believe there'd be the remotest possibility of danger. But a second opinion, a second person's impression of the place and the people, would certainly be valuable.'

The telephone rang, and Maree's concerned voice said, 'Brooke, what is it? Are you all right?'

Brooke told her briefly of the intruders and their threat. 'The police said you should come here and stay, and I agree.'

'But that's silly!' Maree objected. 'I mean, of course I'll come and stay with you for company, but those creeps have no reason to harm *me*. And how could they know where I live? You needn't worry about me.'

'How did they know where *I* live?' Brooke countered. 'Your private address is in the phone directory, just the same way your business address is. And though they have nothing against you, they think for some reason you're my sister, so they're using the threat against you as a lever on me, to make me tell them whatever under heaven it is they want to know, because they don't believe I can't tell them. Oh, Maree, for heaven's sake, don't argue. Just *come*.'

'All right, Brooke,' Maree said quietly, hearing the strung out nervous tension at near-breaking point in her friend's voice. 'I'll be there in fifteen minutes.'

5

Maree stayed for a week, in which both had better locks and exterior sensor-lights installed in their homes, though Maree clearly felt Brooke was over-reacting to the threats of the balaclavas. It was a week when Tom Alford took them both to dinner, and Brooke and Dean Pollock visited his home and drew up landscaping plans for his approval, and the balaclavas didn't return. Neither did the police.

On Saturday afternoon Tom drove Brooke along the modest gravel road through natural bushland and forest that led to the 'New Day Community — Visitors Welcome', as proclaimed by simple block lettering on a white sign where an access road turned off from the public road and led through open farmland where cattle grazed, past several acres of fruit-trees, to a little cluster of functional but not too spartan buildings.

Beyond, more acres of fruit-trees sloped down to a large dam, while a closer, smaller dam was dotted with waterfowl. Near the residential cottages there was a tennis-court and a swimming-pool — none of it lavish, none of it anything but neat and well kept. Two couples were playing mixed doubles on the tennis-court, a couple of adults and several children were in the pool, clearly enjoying it, because the early-October sun was quite hot. A young woman was weeding a vegetable garden, someone was mowing a lawn, and distantly a tractor was spreading fertilizer.

'Doesn't look too fearsome,' Brooke observed drily.

Tom grinned. 'Certainly nothing like I expected. Which was probably something of a cross between boot-camp and monastically severe simplicity.'

There were half a dozen small, timber cottages, four larger concrete-block buildings reminiscent of barracks but appearing to consist of a row of individual rooms, a fair-sized hall and a chapel, with farm sheds at a little distance.

'My preconceptions have certainly just done a back-flip,' Brooke said frankly as Tom stopped the car in front of a room marked 'Office' on the end of one of the larger buildings.

As they got out of the car a tall, lean man with calm blue eyes came out of the office and greeted them with a smile.

'Hello. Are you lost, or have you come to

114

visit us?' His manner was perfectly pleasant.

'Visiting, actually, if that's allowed. We should have phoned,' Tom said apologetically.

'Goodness, visitors are always welcome. Is there anything in particular you wanted to know about our group? I'm George Macintosh, by the way — mostly called Brother George here. I'm not terribly sure how that started, actually, but it seems an established habit now.' He hesitated, looking from one to the other. 'Are you from the press?'

'No.' Tom shook his head. 'I'm Tom Alford. I teach at Broadfell Primary School. This is Mrs Hardwick.'

Interest sharpened instantly in George Macintosh's eyes. 'Mrs Hardwick. Mrs Damien Hardwick?'

Brooke nodded. 'My husband had visited here several times, I believe. He was very interested in your work, especially your anti-drug stance and your rehabilitation work. I felt I'd like to come and see for myself. But we don't want to disturb you.'

Brother George's eyes twinkled. 'And what you've seen so far is not quite what you expected? Not what you'd expect from a bunch of religious weirdos running away from the real world?'

Brooke smiled, finding his easy good-humour infectious. 'Frankly, no.'

He was instantly serious. 'We were very distressed, here, to learn of your husband's death. He was a charming young man, and I believe he was doing much work in trying to educate young people to say no to drugs. Have the police made an arrest yet over his death?'

'No.'

'To be gunned down because you disturb a petty thief . . . ' George Macintosh shook his head sadly. Then he seemed to collect his thoughts. 'But what am I thinking of, keeping you standing in the sun? Come in, come in.'

He led the way through a small, neat office to a sitting-room beyond, simply but comfortably furnished with easy chairs, a couple of small tables, and many bookshelves, well stocked with what appeared to be a wide variety of books. He waved them to chairs.

'Make yourselves comfortable. I'm sure you'd enjoy a cold drink. It's very warm for early October. Perhaps we're heading into a hot summer.'

He disappeared into another room, while Brooke sat in an easy chair and wondered why on earth she had ever imagined for a moment that she could learn anything about her balaclava-clad visitors — or anything that might offer a faint clue to Damien's death — by coming here.

Tom prowled quietly, reading book-titles with an expressionless face, and in a few minutes Brother George came back with a tray and three glasses of fresh orange-juice, ice clinking.

'Now,' George Macintosh said smilingly as they all settled themselves into chairs, frosted glasses in hand, 'how can I help you? You did come for a real reason, I presume?'

'That's perfectly true,' Brooke said, 'but I'm not entirely sure how to explain without sounding either offensive or stupid.'

He looked at her alertly. Tom looked at her with some apprehension.

'Mrs Hardwick,' George Macintosh said gently, 'do you have a drug problem, or know someone who has? We can't provide the professional help someone in that situation needs. We can only help motivate someone who has taken the initial steps to recovery, and feels he or she needs to be away from mainstream life for a time. We're not a drug-rehabilitation centre.'

Brooke stared at him. 'Did my husband tell you I had a drug problem?'

'He said he didn't know, but he feared you may have.'

'I don't.' Brooke found it hard to keep the anger out of her voice. 'I am aware that my husband did suggest to some people that I had a problem. We were not happy together. Drugs were not the problem, and that is not why I'm here.'

She paused. Brother George said simply, 'I'm glad.'

Brooke's anger evaporated. It would always be difficult, she thought wryly, to stay angry with George Macintosh for long. The man radiated a gentle sincerity.

'Mr Macintosh, my husband was not killed by a casual thief. His murder was almost certainly premeditated. Recently, two men broke into my house and threatened me with dire consequences if I didn't tell them where something — presumably drugs — was hidden. Something my husband knew about, they said. Did he — I know this sounds a ridiculous question — did he ever mention to you that he had confiscated from someone a quantity — I gather a large quantity — of hard drugs?'

Brother George looked genuinely astounded. 'No, I assure you. I admit that in the course of his anti-drug work with young people he could have found drugs, and removed them, I suppose, both to prevent the owner or owners from using them and to avoid handing the users over to the police. But he never mentioned . . . wait. Yes, he did tell me once that he had taken some cocaine from a young lad and flushed it down the toilet. Which I'm certain he'd have done with any drugs he found.'

Not, Brooke thought grimly, if he wanted to keep a supply that he could swear was mine.

George Macintosh studied her thoughtfully for a moment. 'Do you think he may have been suspected of having drugs because of his association with this community?' He spread his hands as if to stop any comment, and added with a rueful smile, 'People wonder about us, 'that bunch of nutters in the valley — probably a cover for a drug business', I'm well aware of some of the things that are said about us. If that misconception was the reason someone invaded your home, I'm sincerely sorry. But I give you my word we are not involved with drugs here.'

Tom said, 'Can you guarantee that Damien Hardwick would never have found someone here in possession of drugs — heroin, cocaine, something like that?'

The older man frowned, and sighed. 'No, I can't give a hard-and-fast guarantee on anything. This isn't a prison-farm. People are free to come and go, to live their own lives, within certain rules. Those rules include no drugs except prescription drugs, no alcohol, no smoking. Break those rules more than once and you must leave. The rules run on a sort of honour system, which actually works surprisingly well. But they only apply on the property. If someone goes out to work, as some residents do, obviously there's no control over what they do while away from the community. Again, there's rarely any hint of trouble.'

He looked from Tom to Brooke. 'I would tell you, if I knew,' he said simply.

Brooke stood up. 'Yes. I believe you. I'm sorry to have intruded.'

George Macintosh stood also. 'Please, it isn't an intrusion. Not knowing who murdered your husband, or exactly why, must be very cruel.' He walked with them to the door and said with enthusiasm, 'I would love to show you a little of our work here, if you can spare the time.'

Brooke and Tom said they could, and he proceeded to show them around the buildings, introducing them here and there to some of the residents.

'I was a minister in the Baptist church,' he explained. 'My wife was in an accident caused by a drunken driver. She died. My life was shattered. All I wanted was to go and hide from the world, coward that I am. My grandfather had been a reasonably wealthy man who bequeathed me a considerable sum of money. This place had been someone's ill-conceived idea of establishing a holiday-farm, but it's in the wrong place for such a venture.' He stooped down to pull a weed beside the path.

'It was up for sale and I bought it with the thought in my mind that there must be many shattered people like myself, shattered by many different circumstances — who needed somewhere to retreat, either permanently or just until they could find the strength to go back into the world. I thought such a venture might give my own life some purpose which I couldn't find in my normal routine. I thought maybe this was a better way to serve God and my fellow-humans than by preaching sermons.'

He flashed them a sudden grin. 'I wasn't much of a preacher, anyway. So, this gradually developed. Some people live here permanently, working the place. We have three hundred acres of land, some leased to an adjoining farmer to run cattle on, some under avocados and nectarines on a commercial scale as well as fruit and vegetables for ourselves. People . . . '

A little shadow fell across his face. 'People come here for many sad reasons. Some have lost family, like myself. Some are picking up the pieces of lives they've damaged themselves with drugs or alcohol. Some have been brutally abused by their partners. And so on. Ah, Don.' He spoke to a stocky man who was weeding a flower-bed. 'I'd like you to meet Mrs Hardwick, Damien's widow.'

The man straightened and looked steadily at Brooke. 'Mrs Hardwick,' he said courteously, and pulled off a gardening glove and shook hands, then turned back abruptly to his weeding.

They walked on. 'Donald was very distressed when your husband was killed,' Brother George said. 'They had become close friends.'

When they said goodbye to George Macintosh and drove away, Tom said, 'Well I don't know about you, but I'd be pretty certain everything about that place is genuine. I didn't expect to feel like that, I admit, and I don't think their way is the way I'd want to cope with the aftermath of personal trauma, but I guess it would certainly fill a need for some.'

'Oh, yes, I agree. I know that you can be hoodwinked by charming rogues, but I can't put Brother George into a villain's role.'

Tom drove for a little while in silence, and then slid a sideways glance at her. 'And yet something there upset you.'

She looked at him quickly. 'Perceptive, aren't you?' She smiled faintly. 'That man who was weeding, the one who was a friend of Damien's. He shook hands, he spoke courteously, even if briefly. And he looked at me with hate in his eyes.'

'Hate!' Tom sounded baffled. 'But — why on earth would he hate you? You must have imagined it.'

Brooke shook her head. 'Even here, there's suspicion. That man thinks I killed Damien.'

Tom pulled over to the side of the road and stopped. 'Brooke,' he said, looking shaken. 'I never quite realized — well, how much you believe people look at you with speculation. I don't believe more than a tiny handful would.'

'Don't you?' There was bitterness in her voice. 'Thank you for believing in me, Tom, though I don't know why you should. And I still have other friends who believe in me, too, thank God.'

She shrugged. 'But suspicion spreads like a malignant virus. I once saw a film called 'Ordeal by Innocence', based on an Agatha Christie mystery novel. It involved a family being torn apart because they knew one of themselves was a murderer, but only the guilty knew which one. So they all suspected each other. At the time I thought how awful it would be for the innocent.' She gave a short laugh. 'I hadn't the remotest idea then of just how awful.'

After a moment Tom said quietly, 'I'm sorry. And that still sounds a trite and inadequate platitude if ever I heard one.'

Brooke shook her head. 'No. Because you mean it and there's nothing else you can say.' She was silent for a moment and then she said slowly, 'I can never quite stop thinking: what if the police never find who killed Damien? How do I cope, going through the rest of my life with people wondering? *That*, for the rest of my life!'

He put a hand for a moment gently over hers. 'It won't be like that. The police will find the truth.'

She said bleakly, 'Thank you, Tom. I just wish I could believe it.'

He thought, as he started the car again: so do I.

6

Dean Pollock, grim-faced, arrived at Brooke's front door just as she was leaving for work a few days after the visit to the New Day community.

At the end of a week of sharing Brooke's rented cottage, Maree had announced firmly that she was going back to her own flat.

'I've loved having your company,' she told Brooke, 'but we've both had some pretty good security put in place. And anyway, I suppose it's partly a matter of principle: I'm not going to let some creep drive me out of my home — even if it is only a one-bedroom flat. Anyway, those thugs would have done something in support of their threats before this, if they'd been serious.'

Brooke herself was feeling increasingly confident that the balaclavas' threats had been a token gesture born of frustration at not being handed the drugs they wanted, or at least being told where they were. She had almost got over feeling the jolt of apprehension she had experienced for the first couple of days every time the phone rang and she would pick it up, her mouth dry, half-expecting a voice to demand what she couldn't give.

But on this morning one look at her junior partner told her something was badly wrong.

'Dean? What is it?'

'The motel job. I had a call from the manager. All the landscaping we did has been vandalized.'

'Oh, no! Mindless low-life! What makes them tick?' Brooke said heatedly. 'Does the manager think it was just mindless vandalism, or someone with a grudge against him?'

'No,' Dean said bitterly. 'He had a phonecall just on daylight. Someone with a grudge against *us*.'

It took a few numbing seconds for the truth to register. 'Not against us, Dean,' she said quietly. 'Against me.'

'Against you is against Greenlands Landscaping, and that's against Dean Pollock, too,' he said. 'I'd like five minutes with the swine.'

Brooke managed a pale-faced smile, touched by his fiery loyalty. 'Thanks, Dean. But we both know it's directed at me. Have you seen it?'

He nodded.

'Bad?'

'Bad.'

'Well, we'd better go take a look.'

Brooke got her own car out of the garage

and followed Dean, who was driving the partnership's one-ton pick-up, to the motel, attractively set on the edge of the village. Or it had been attractive.

A paved driveway curved up from the road to the reception area at the front of the low-set building, and then continued to a paved courtyard parking area. Along the sweep of the driveway, Brooke and Dean had planted small growing conical cypress and azaleas, with massed bedding begonias.

As a screen from adjoining houses on one side they had planted large, native shrubs — callistemons, with their red, bottle-brush flowers loved by birds; and small-type lillypillies, with glossy green leaves, fluffy white flowers and pink fruit.

Nothing was left but chaos.

Plants and shrubs had been torn out of the ground, twisted, broken, trampled, flung across the lawn. Rock walls that had been Dean's pride had been pulled down and the rocks flung on to garden beds and driveway. The motel manager was out, clearing the driveway of its obstructions. He straightened up as Dean and Brooke drove up.

'Done a job of it, haven't they?' he said grimly. 'Mongrels must've worked on it in the early hours of the morning. I closed up the office just before eleven and went to bed. Our living quarters are in behind the office, and we didn't hear a thing. The milkman woke me when he came, to tell me. Then I got the phonecall.'

Brooke said quietly, 'What did he say? Exactly, if you can remember.'

The manager looked uncomfortable. 'Leaving out most of the obscenities, he said, 'If you get that murdering bitch to do any more work for you, you'll get more of the same'. I'm sorry, Mrs Hardwick. I was very pleased with what you did here, but I think he meant what he said. And I can't guard against it.'

Brooke nodded, feeling slightly sick. 'Yes, I dare say he meant what he said. Do you have insurance that will cover this?'

'Yes. But you see, I can't afford — '

'No, of course not,' Brooke cut in quickly. 'You can't afford to have this happen again. We'll clean up the mess for you. I don't think the vandals could object to that. Take some photographs before we start, for the insurance assessor. Then get someone else to re-do the work.'

The manager looked relieved. 'Thanks. And I'm sorry.'

Dean was already piling rocks to one side. 'Keep 'em,' he said tersely. 'The next landscaper can use them.'

It took almost an hour to clear the wrecked

plants off the lawn and the driveway, and they worked in angry silence, piling plants into the back of the utility, raking the small bits off the lawn and sweeping the driveway. Dean stood for a moment beside the cabin of the pick-up, looking back at the now tidy but bare motel gardens.

'What a bloody waste!' he said. 'Do you reckon this was the work of those thugs who broke into your house?'

Brooke shook her head. 'I'd guess it's most unlikely.'

'But who else would want to get at *you*?'

She shrugged. 'Someone who doesn't like to see a murderer sharing a successful business. Or sharing the same town.'

'That's bullshit!' Dean snapped. 'No one in their right mind could think you're a murderer.'

'Then I'm afraid there must be a lot of people around Broadfell with mental problems.'

He stared at her. 'Are you saying other things have happened?'

'Little things. Not like this.' She had never talked with her young partner about the suspicion touching her.

'I'd like to smash their teeth!' His red hair seemed to positively bristle.

Brooke smiled wryly. 'But, Dean, what else

can I expect? What are people to think? I'll bet you've heard rumours that I use drugs. Everyone knows Damien hated drugs. So there we have a motive, if I was addicted and he tried to stop me. In actual fact it was Damien himself who started the rumour about me and drugs, and he threatened to plant drugs on me if I left him.'

Dean stared, shocked. 'Hell!' he said. 'Bloody hell!'

'But there's only my word for that. And who would be more familiar with where he kept the shot-gun? Who would be most easily able to go into the house without arousing his suspicions? The police obviously think I killed him. Why wouldn't other people think the same? Haven't the police questioned you about my movements on that day? You didn't know what I did, or when, because you were out on a job. But they've asked, haven't they?'

He looked furious and miserable at the same time. 'Well, yeah. Okay, yeah. *And* they asked if I thought you used heroin or cocaine or stuff like that, and I told them they had rocks in their heads. I know what the hard stuff does to people, I know how they behave. And I know bloody well you never touch the stuff. I'm sorry, boss. I had no idea things were that bad.'

Brooke simply nodded and touched his

arm. 'Thank you. Now we'd better get back to work. If you take that truck-load of wreckage to the rubbish-tip, I'll go around to the nursery and check on some of the things that would go well in Tom Alford's garden.'

'Yeah.' He stood for a moment, clearly wanting to say more, but for once in his cheerful life lost for words. 'Yeah, sure.' He climbed up into the cabin of the pick-up and drove away.

Brooke drove out to the nursery, a concrete-block building which housed the office and the covered area for indoor plants and plant containers, fertilizers and potting-mix. At the back, the building opened out on to the extensive area of varied plants for sale, some under shade-cloth, some out in the open, according to the sort of environment they needed. The whole was enclosed behind a three-metre, sturdy wire-mesh fence with gates which were locked when the nursery was closed.

As Brooke stopped in the sealed parking area in front of the building, Barnaby Woods and his daughter, Jenny — who both worked for Patricia with the same sort of transparent pleasure in their work that Dean brought to Greenlands Landscaping — were loading some wilted plants into the nursery van.

Instant apprehension grabbed Brooke's

131

stomach. There were perhaps thirty assorted plants in pots ready for sale — fruit-trees, azaleas, camellias, hibiscus, some native rain forest plants — all drooping and clearly dying.

'Barnaby! What's happened to them?'

'They've been sprayed with herbicide — Zero, or some such. Hard to say when — a few nights ago, probably. It takes a while for the effects to show.'

'You think it was deliberate?' Even as she asked the question, she knew the answer.

'Yep,' he said. ' 'Fraid so.'

Jenny said bitterly, 'We know it was deliberate, Mrs Hardwick. Patricia had a phonecall.'

Brooke closed her eyes, feeling sick. 'Let me guess. The caller said that if the nursery did any more business with me, next time it would be worse.'

Neither Barnaby nor Jenny answered.

Brooke nodded. 'I see. But how was this done? Did someone break through the fence, or the gate?'

'There wasn't any need, when he just wanted to knock a few plants as a — well, a sort of warning. These were all growing near the fence. Easy enough to spray weedkiller on to them from outside.'

'When did the warning call come?' Brooke

asked. 'Just this morning?'

'Yesterday,' Barnaby said. 'I took the call. Thought it was just some crank, because the damage hadn't shown up at that stage. I just told him where to go.'

Jenny looked keenly at Brooke. 'How did you guess it was about you, Mrs Hardwick?'

Brooke told them about the motel gardens. 'It seems someone has taken it on himself to drive me and my contaminating influence out of Broadfell by sabotaging everyone who does business with me.'

Her voice was unsteady with anger and she turned and went across to the office. Patricia looked up from some paperwork and came quickly around the desk to give Brooke a wordless hug.

Brooke sighed and sat on a corner of the desk-cum-shop-counter. 'I'm sorry, Pat.'

Patricia shook her head. 'Don't be silly. It's nothing to do with you. Don't look like that.'

'But it does involve me. But for me, this wouldn't have happened, and the threat wouldn't be hanging over you.'

'It's only bluff.'

'I don't think so.' She told Patricia what had happened at the motel. 'You can't risk doing business with me. This nut could ruin you. You have thousands — a good many thousands of dollars worth of plants here. He

— or they — don't even have to cut through the fence. All they need do is choose a nice windy night to carry the spray, and they can virtually wipe you out. I'll try buying plants I need elsewhere, and work as anonymously as I can. If anyone anywhere is prepared to take the risk of giving me work to do.'

Patricia said heatedly, 'No one is going to tell me who I can and can't sell to! You're far and away my best customer.'

Brooke shook her head and slid wearily off the desk to her feet. 'And one who'll ruin you if you continue to deal with me. Obviously I can't do any local work. I'll just have to look for work down at the coast, or — '

She stopped abruptly. 'Oh, Lord,' she said softly.

'What?' Patricia demanded concernedly. 'What is it?'

'The Blue Crystal Waters tender. Dean and I have put a lot of work into planning for that. We think we have a good chance of winning the contract. Sorry — *thought* we had. But if this noble character who wants me out of town knows about it — and we haven't made any particular secret of the fact we're submitting a tender — the developers aren't going to risk giving us the job and then seeing it wrecked.'

'Brooke!' Patricia looked distressed. 'Surely

that wouldn't happen.'

Brooke stood leaning back against the desk, staring unseeingly at plant containers and bags of potting-mix. Cold defeat was swamping her mind.

'I vowed I wouldn't let suspicion drive me out of Broadfell,' she said flatly. 'I'd ride it out. I believed the police would find the truth, in the end, and everything would be all right for me. But I'm not sure I can believe that any more. And this — probably just one person — may very well finish me.'

She turned and looked at her friend with an attempt at a smile. 'Sorry, Pat. I'm just being sorry for myself.'

She walked out quickly and drove away.

Dean Pollock had just driven into the yard as she arrived. He looked hard at her, taking in the tenseness in the set of her jaw, the pale face, the look of stunned defeat.

'Hey, boss,' he said with surprising gentleness. 'We'll just put that one down to experience. OK?'

'It might be,' Brooke said very quietly, 'except that there's been another.'

'*What?*'

She told him. 'The warning's out, Dean, and it's very clear. Do business with Greenlands Landscaping and I'll ruin you. But the true objective, of course, is to ruin me. The rotten part is, it'll drag you under with the wreckage, and it's nothing to do with you. I'll have to sell my share of the business, if I can find a buyer.'

'Because of one sanctimonious bastard who wants to be judge, jury and executioner without a shred of evidence? Brooke! Are you out of your *tree*? Call the cops! *He's* the lawbreaker, not you. You have a right to be protected, and so have the people he's threatened. What he's doing is a kind of extortion.'

'Dean, the police would probably rather give him a medal than take him to court. And how many vandals are ever caught?'

'Give him a taste of being hunted, though. Otherwise you're just letting him get away with it.'

She hesitated listlessly, and he said, 'Aw, come on. Do it for uncle, eh?'

She smiled in spite of herself. 'All right. But it's not really up to me to take it to the police. The motel people and Patricia are the appropriate ones to call in the law. I'd have to approach them about it.'

'Right. You call Pat Evans and I'll go and talk to the motel manager.'

Patricia readily agreed when Brooke phoned her. 'I had thought about calling the police,' she told Brooke, 'but it seemed trivial.

136

I realize now, of course, that it isn't trivial at all, because it's aimed at ruining you.'

Dean came back to report that the motel manager had already not only notified the police, but had taken photographs of the damage before Dean and Brooke had started cleaning up, and he had given the photos to the local newspaper. They had sent a reporter, who had still been at the motel when Dean arrived, and Dean had sent him around to the nursery to talk to Patricia.

The police, when they came to see Brooke and Dean, asked who would have a grudge against Greenlands Landscaping, looked non-committal and said glumly that the chances of catching vandals were not good.

The newspaper obligingly ran a small story, and Tom Alford angrily rejected Brooke's suggestion that he should get someone else to do his landscaping.

'No one is going to tell me who I can engage to do professional work for me. I asked you and Dean to do this job, and you and Dean are the ones I want to do it. I like the design you worked out, and I want you to do the work, and no one is going to tell me I can't have my own garden the way I want it.'

He and Brooke had been standing in the front yard of his home, looking across the still-raw newness of the garden area where so far nothing had been planted and only a path of terra-cotta-coloured pavers leading to the front door, and the driveway of similar material, broke the harshness of the bare earth. The house stood a little back from the edge of the escarpment, where the Blackall Range plunged steeply down a couple of hundred metres to farmland and, beyond, past small towns to the distant, misty blue of the Pacific, all bathed in the golden light of an October late afternoon.

Tom turned abruptly to Brooke. 'There's a rather pleasant entertainment evening next Saturday, in the local hall,' he said. 'A professional group — singers, a couple of instrumentalists and a magician. They do part of their programme directed at children, hence the magician, I guess, and they like local children involved, so the school choir will do a couple of items. The rest of the programme covers most musical tastes. I've heard these people before, and they're rather good. Would you come with me? Please?'

Brooke looked at him, her face soft. 'That's very kind of you, Tom, but it won't do you any good to be seen with me. I've explained that.'

His eyes glinted with swift anger. 'I just told you that no one is going to tell me who can and who can't landscape my garden, and

I'm damned if anyone's going to tell me who my friends can be.'

Brooke closed her eyes for a moment. 'Tom,' she said quietly, 'you're the kindest man I ever met. But you're a teacher — I suspect a very good one — and I've told you before that parents rightly demand certain standards from the people who spend time with their children. I'm a murder-suspect. Certainly, thank God, there are friends who have total faith in me, regardless of the way the evidence points. That doesn't change the simple fact: I'm a murder-suspect. Your career's involved here. Don't tarnish it by being seen socially with me.'

He stepped forward and put his hands on her shoulders. 'You are not a murderer. Whoever killed your husband did so with premeditated, calm deliberation. You could never coldly and calculatedly kill.'

'You don't know me well enough to know that.'

'Wrong. I do know you well enough. And I would be proud to be seen with you anywhere. Please come to the concert with me.' His eyes were serious. 'Please. It's important to me.'

She studied his face for a long moment. 'I think you're mad,' she said very quietly. 'But very well, thank you, I'll come.'

He smiled with clear pleasure. 'Good.' He turned and his glance ran over the house, his expression contented. 'You know, once the garden is set up, I'd like a couple of animals — a puppy and a kitten or two. The fence is puppy proof, and I think it would be a good place for animals. What do you think?'

Brooke nodded. 'I should think any animals living here would be very happy. Now I must get back to the office.'

Tom walked with her to her car. 'I'll see you on Saturday evening. The concert starts early, due to the fact the first part is principally for children. so I'll pick you up a little before seven.'

She smiled at him. 'Thank you.'

Neither of them could have had the faintest premonition that when Saturday evening was over, a number of things would have changed in Broadfell.

* * *

The day was unusually hot for that time of the year, and through the afternoon a few storm-heads had pushed piles of curdled white cloud high into the south-western sky, but all had either broken up or slid away to the south, with no more than an occasional distant drum-roll of thunder, though the air was still warm and humid with the promise of much-needed rain, as Tom and Brooke arrived at the hall.

Other cars were arriving, with most of the occupants clearly knowing Tom, obviously other teachers and parents. It was equally clear that he was popular with everyone. And equally clear that most people were uncomfortable at meeting him with Brooke. Tom seemed totally unaware of it, and cheerfully introduced her.

He greeted one couple with, 'Hi, Barry, Angela. Brooke, I'd like you to meet my boss, Barry Endicott and his wife Angela. Barry's the primary-school principal and Angela teaches also. This is Brooke Hardwick.'

The murmured greeting, like others, was polite, but the smiles were suddenly rather wooden, and a quick remark about the weather and 'We'd better get to our seats' was the extent of convivial conversation. Brooke fervently wished she was at home reading a book, but she was committed to the evening now, and could only embarrass Tom by not following his lead and behaving as though nothing was amiss.

As they walked towards the hall from where Tom had parked the car in the street, he said, 'Normally there's some parking space at the side of the hall, near that tree, but we had to rope it off because the ground's absolutely saturated and boggy there. Some clown left an outside tap turned on, from the hall rainwater tank would you believe, and drained nearly ten thousand gallons out before anyone noticed the water running down the gutters and came to investigate. We had to get a water-tanker in this morning to refill the tank for the toilets and so on.'

Brooke smiled. 'That poor old gum tree beside the fence will think the wet season's come early.'

'It might get even wetter,' Tom commented. 'There are storms forecast for tomorrow, and it's certainly been pretty hot today.'

'A storm sounds like a good idea,' Brooke said. 'It's ages now since we had good rain. Things are beginning to look wilted.'

They found themselves seats near the front entrance, at the further end from the stage, but gratefully beside a window, left open to admit such breeze as there was.

No doubt partly because of the involvement of local children, the concert had attracted an audience big enough to almost fill the hall, but Brooke was painfully aware that the seats near theirs were slow to fill. Several people came, glanced at them, and moved to other seats. There were, of course, exceptions. Patricia and Cameron deliberately sought them out, and a few other friends and some scant acquaintances behaved no differently from normal. And slowly the seats filled for the simple reason they were the only ones left.

The concert opened with a couple of songs by a young woman who had a guitar and a charming voice. She was followed by the magician, who involved as many children from the audience as possible, keeping them entranced and delighted. Brooke felt herself relaxing. All eyes were on the stage now, and the presence of a murder-suspect in the audience was forgotten. A cooling breeze had sprung up, and as it fanned in gently through the open window she found she could lose herself for the moment in the simple pleasure of watching the performance. A little desultory, distant thunder added the welcome hint of a possible shower later.

After the magician, the compere, Colin Paton, who was a church elder and had been a staunch admirer of Damien Hardwick, announced that the next item on the programme would be a series of songs presented by the choir of the Broadfell Primary School. Watching him smilingly ushering the children on to the stage, Brooke felt a twist of the grief which was always there, deep inside her like an ulcer that wouldn't heal — grief for the friendships and the trust which Damien's murderer had taken from her.

Colin Paton and his wife were pleasant, kind, intelligent people whom she had regarded as friends. They operated a real-estate business and had two children — both of whom, she noticed as the choir, neat in their school uniforms, filed on to the stage, were choir members. Since Damien's death the Patons, even the children, had studiously avoided her. They had been among the people in whose minds Damien had planted the seeds of suspicion that she was on hard drugs. She couldn't blame them for their attitude towards her. But it hurt.

As the children assembled on the stage, two of the teachers — the conductor and the accompanist, a pianist — took their places in front of the stage at floor level.

Tom whispered with a grin, 'This is all thoroughly ecumenical. The compère's an Anglican; Beverly Sheehan, the conductor, is a practising Catholic; and Doris Maddox the pianist doesn't believe in anything.'

Intent on her thoughts, Brooke hadn't noticed until that moment that the breeze had freshened and there had been some slightly closer thunder, but a sudden flash of

144

brilliant lightning and close-following crack of thunder announced that a storm was coming up quickly. Tom stood up to close the window.

'Hope it doesn't rain too heavily,' he whispered. 'The kids — and parents, too — are going to be awfully disappointed if they can't be heard properly, and heavy rain would make quite a racket on this iron roof.'

'It's coming up so quickly it should blow over quickly,' Brooke whispered back.

The pianist played the lead-in bars, and the clear, young voices launched into a joyful chorus.

Three near flashes of lightning followed in rapid succession, and Tom whispered, 'If there was a vocal version, the *Eighteen-twelve Overture* would go well. The cannon are firing.'

Brooke smiled, and then suddenly tensed. 'Tom! Listen!'

He listened, frowning slightly. 'Sounds like the wind getting up a bit.'

Brooke sprang up. 'More than a bit. It's bad. Tom, the tree! Those children have to come off the stage. The ground's soaked around that tree. If it comes down, that's where it will hit.'

Heads were turning angrily, with, 'Shh! Shhhh!'

Brooke shouted, running forward toward the stage with Tom, looking slightly bewildered, close behind, 'Get those children off the stage! Now! There's a tree may fall on that end of the hall.'

There was a general mutter of annoyance, a few calls of 'Sit down! Be quiet!' The children, startled, straggled into silence, staring at the woman who was running down the aisle. The pianist carried on for a few bars, but the conductor turned uncertainly, and Colin Paton, the compere, blocked Brooke's path.

'What do you think you're doing, you stupid bitch?' he shouted, his face dark with rage.

'Get the children off the stage!' Brooke shouted in reply. 'Get out of my way!'

Colin Paton caught at her arm, but Tom shoved him violently aside. '*Listen*!' he snapped. 'Listen, can't you?'

The ominous roar which Brooke had detected moments earlier was sweeping closer on a frightening crescendo.

'Everyone! Get away from the stage area! Go!' Tom yelled. Then he and Brooke and the conductor were up on the stage, herding bewildered children down the steps to the body of the hall.

'Go toward the door but don't go outside!'

Brooke was urging, shouting above the sound of storm-carried menace.

Not entirely sure what the problem was, but recognizing that Brooke and Tom were desperately concerned, the school principal and the pianist joined in shepherding children away from the stage. With a blinding white flash and an instant crash of thunder the lights went out, and in the same moment the wind hit, driving rain and hail with deafening violence against the building till the old weather-board hall shuddered under the battering.

Dimly, Brooke was aware that some children were screaming in terror, their voices barely audible above the storm. She and Tom ushered the last of the choir members off the stage and Tom hurried them away from it, working by the light of the blazing swords of lightning that stabbed the wild blackness.

Brooke glanced back at the stage and saw one little girl of perhaps eight, crouched at the back of the stage with her hands over her face, frozen in panic. Brooke heard a man beside her shout, 'Simone!' and she and he ran back on to the stage together.

At that moment there was another sound — a tearing, splintering crash far louder than even the worst thunder-clap. Brooke had just time to realize that the tree had come down, and then everything around her was splintering, wrenching timber and iron and branches in a deafening cacophony of destruction, and for a split second she felt a vicious pain in her leg, and blackness swallowed her.

★ ★ ★

The first thing she became aware of was continuing noise — wind and thunder mixed in a conglomerate of sound, punctuated by shouts which were only faintly heard above the storm. She was wet and she was cold, which seemed ludicrous, because it had been so hot. And wet? Why was she wet? And something clammily wet was in her face. It felt like leaves, but that was absurd. There were flashing white lights, flaring blindingly even behind closed eyelids, and then vanishing into the blackness that rushed after them like a wave sweeping up the beach.

Perhaps if she could open her eyes she could tell what was going on, but it was too much trouble. She lifted one hand to feel the wet things against her face.

They *were* leaves. And in that instant consciousness came back, and she realized she must have been unconscious for no more than a few moments.

The tree had come down, and she was

under the branches. Carefully she tried moving, and with a rush of relief found legs and arms all functioned, and she was entangled in light branches, not pinned by crushing weight.

But wind-driven rain and hail lashed at her and she put one arm over her face just as Tom's voice beside her shouted 'Brooke! Brooke! Are you hurt? Don't try to move.'

He turned his head and called, 'There's someone trapped here! Has anyone got a torch?'

A couple of men scrambled forward and, working by the dazzle of brilliant lightning and pitch darkness in alternate bursts, two of them eased the branches away from Brooke while Tom and another man carefully slid their arms under her and, supporting her spine, lifted her clear. She recognized Barry Endicott, the school principal.

'I'm all right,' she insisted, and they helped her stand.

'The little girl!' she cried in horror as memory surged back. 'She was over by the wall.'

The hail had stopped, but the wind still howled through what the lightning flashes revealed to be the wreckage of that end of the hall, and rain drove with stinging force. The top half of the eucalypt tree had demolished

149

the roof and the side-wall, and the whole wreckage lay in a great heap of shattered timber and roofing iron.

'What little girl?' Barry Endicott demanded anxiously.

'She was over there.' Brooke pointed. 'Against the wall. Oh, God.'

She started to claw her way across the wreckage, but Tom grabbed her. 'No!' he shouted. 'You're hurt. Stay here.'

Several other people had struggled through the wreckage that was scattered up the aisles, and Maree gripped Brooke's arm. The men were clambering over the tangled debris.

Almost as quickly as it had come, the wind was dropping and the rain was easing, and the sound of a siren wailed closer.

'There's someone trapped here!' one of the men said sharply.

Someone clambered to him with a torch, and there was a long moment of silence.

'It's Colin,' the first man said in a shaken voice. 'Colin Paton.'

The sound of the storm had dropped enough for his words to carry through the hall.

'Colin!' a woman cried in fear. 'Is he — hurt?'

'He's — he's unconscious,' the man who had found him said.

150

Brooke didn't know whether Dianne Paton guessed the truth that lay behind the attempted kindness of that answer.

'He was with me,' Brooke said. 'We both saw the little girl and started back for her just as the tree fell.'

Blue flashing lights outside told that a police car had come, and another torchlight swept the wreckage as the only local policeman came into the hall. Someone was holding Dianne Paton.

'Down this end,' one of the rescuers from the audience called. 'There's a man — trapped — and a little girl here somewhere.'

'There are ambulances on their way, and more officers, and the State Emergency Service people,' the policeman said as he began to scramble and claw his way across the stage, his torch making the grim search easier, especially as now, with the storm racing away to the north-east, the lightning was already less bright.

'She's here!' Tom called. 'She's all right. Nearly, anyway, aren't you, sweetheart?'

A ragged cheer went round the hall.

Brooke had been vaguely aware that Maree was holding her arm, and now she realized Patricia and Cameron were beside her also, as was another woman, shaking violently.

'I can't find my little girl! It must be her. It

must be. I can't find her!' Terror filled her voice.

Brooke was feeling unaccountably dizzy. She tried to focus her mind on the woman's anguish. 'What — what's your little girl's name?'

'Simone,' the woman said. 'I've looked . . . '

'That's Simone,' Brooke said. 'That's what Colin called her.'

And with total abruptness darkness and silence rolled over her for the second time that night, and Patricia and Maree caught her as she fell.

★ ★ ★

The rest of the night was a confused blur for Brooke. She had a muddled recollection of being loaded into an ambulance while a voice which sounded somehow familiar but which she didn't realize was her own, kept saying, 'I don't need to go to hospital. I'm all right. Tom will take me home.' A hospital bed. An oxygen mask. Someone saying something about X-rays and something about blood. There'd been an oxygen mask in the ambulance, too. Trolleys, and being wheeled somewhere, and then oblivion.

The morning saw daylight clear and bright outside her hospital window, and last night's storm could have been a bad dream, except that her mind had cleared and she was perfectly aware that it was no dream. Her head ached horribly and one leg hurt and she felt her whole body was covered in bruises.

A nurse came in cheerfully, took her temperature and told her, in answer to her questions, that the doctor would soon be in and he'd fill her in on what had happened, but she was doing fine.

The doctor was tall, grey-haired and had an easy smile.

'Why am I here?' Brooke demanded. 'Why did I faint last night?'

'You'd had a whack on the head that caused concussion and we had to check for a skull fracture — fortunately there wasn't one, but you probably feel as if you've a dandy hangover. Your leg had been cut by flying glass-splinters and we had to remove a few bits of glass before we sewed you up. You'd lost a lot of blood. I gather that in the darkness and with everything else that was happening up there, no one noticed for quite a while just how much you were bleeding.'

'How many other people were hurt?'

He hesitated a moment. 'We have three in here, but no one's badly hurt. Bad cuts and bruises, a couple of broken ribs, and shock. Mainly in overnight for observation.'

'The little girl — Simone? Is she here?'

'Yes. But she's fine, only shocked, a couple of fairly minor cuts, and a broken toe.'

Brooke shuddered. 'When I looked back, and saw her, and heard the tree begin to fall . . .'

The doctor put his hand on her shoulder. 'She's fine,' he repeated. 'You'll all be going home today. It was a rough experience, but life goes on.'

'Not for Colin Paton, though, does it?' she asked quietly.

He looked at her levelly. 'I believe one man lost his life,' he said gently. 'I don't know the details.'

Tom came for her.

'Tom! This is kind of you. Somehow I expected Maree or Patricia when they told me a friend had come to take me home.'

He smiled. His face was lined with weariness. 'Maree's place was damaged. Patricia's helping her clean it up.'

She didn't ask any more questions until he had helped her into the car and stowed the crutches she would need for a few days, in the back seat.

Then she said steadily as he drove out of town and toward the range, 'Was Colin Paton killed outright?'

He flicked her a sidelong glance. 'How did

you know he was dead?'

'I guessed, from the way the man who found him spoke.'

Tom nodded. 'He wouldn't have known what hit him, poor fellow.'

'And the little girl was safe all the time. Dianne — his wife — will feel he died for nothing.'

'He didn't, though, did he?' Tom said. 'He couldn't guess, and neither could you, and you both went to try to save her — he couldn't guess that some freak of chance, or act of God or whatever you like to call it, would mean that the tree-limbs and the roof pieces could come down all around her, and the end wall deflect them just enough to miss her. He didn't die for nothing. He died trying to save a child's life, and nothing can take that away from him.' He looked at her again. 'And it can't change the fact you got hurt trying to save her, too.'

Brooke was silent for a moment. 'Ironic, isn't it? If we'd had enough time to get to her and start to take her off the stage, she'd probably have been killed, too. She lived because our rescue bid failed.'

Tom said sharply, 'Don't talk like that. Don't think like that! That doesn't take anything from your courage or Colin Paton's. Just remember that.'

She said slowly, 'Poor Colin. He and Dianne used to be friends of ours — Damien's and mine — and he died hating me because he believed I killed Damien.'

Tom took one hand off the wheel for a moment and put it on her arm. 'What he believed isn't your fault.'

Neither spoke for a little while, and then she gave herself a little shake. 'What else happened, Tom? In Broadfell? Was anywhere else damaged — any other districts, I mean?'

'Apparently it was just a very narrow strip, tornado style, even if not a full-fledged twister. Broadfell seems to be the only area hit, and only part of that. About a third of the hall is totally beyond repair, four houses were totally unroofed, another tree fell on a car, several other houses and some businesses had varying degrees of other damage — partial roof-loss, windows smashed by hail and so on — and there are trees down and limbs ripped off trees everywhere, and a lot of hail damage to cars. This one was lucky, mainly protected by the fact I had parked it partly under the awning of the shop near the hall. Your house is okay, so is mine. Gardens are pretty well stripped by hail, but they'll re-grow. Patricia's nursery missed the worst of it.'

'You said Maree's place had been damaged. How badly?'

'The building isn't damaged. It's the interior.' There was a grimness in his voice. 'It wasn't the storm.'

'Wasn't the storm? What . . . ?' She stopped, a new sickening wave of dismay clutching at her. 'You mean they came back? Those thugs? The balaclavas?'

'Apparently. Someone did. Broke in and made quite a mess of the inside of the shop. They'd come through the back, away from the street. Maree didn't know until this morning when she went along early to check if there'd been any damage from the storm.'

Brooke put her face in her hands. 'Poor Maree! I thought — hoped — they'd come to accept that I didn't know anything about the damned drugs. If they ever existed. I'd really begun to believe I'd never hear of them again.'

She shivered. 'Tom, what can I do? What else will they do?'

He touched her arm again. 'Try not to worry too much. This will possibly give the police a chance to trace them. It also may make the police a bit keener to try tracing them than before, when all the creeps had done was threaten. This, now, is clear extortion, and the fact that your balaclava friends would go this far suggests the stuff they're after is a good-sized haul. But I guess you can expect a call from the balaclava men, unfortunately. Somehow, though, I can't see them doing anything else. Once they find you won't tell them anything now, I really believe they'll accept that you told them the truth: you don't know where the stuff is. Or even, as you say, if it exists.'

She took a long breath. 'Dear heaven, Tom, it's only a few hours since we were peacefully going to a concert. Now buildings are wrecked, a man is dead, people are hurt, and cowardly criminals have vandalized an inno-cent person's livelihood. Poor Broadfell.'

The road that had wound up the range in sweeping, tree-edged curves with glimpses of farmland below, levelled out and Tom turned toward the village.

'Destruction isn't the only thing which has happened overnight in Broadfell,' he said. 'I think you'll find a lot of people who might have cold-shouldered you yesterday have had to do some rethinking.'

'What do you mean?'

'You realized long before anyone else that there was a real danger — that the storm was extraordinary, and the tree could come down on the stage-end of the hall.'

'Only because you'd told me about the water from the tank.'

He shook his head. 'Broadfell is in some

shock this morning, and in grief for a man's life lost. But think: if that tree had fallen with thirty children on the stage, the tragedy would have been hideous. Broadfell has to thank you for its children.'

'That's nonsense. The danger wouldn't have occurred to me if you hadn't told me about that tap being left on, and the ground being so sodden. And once, when I was a teenager on the farm, we had a storm come through that made a roar like that. So I knew last night it was going to be bad. But I couldn't have got the children away from that end of the hall if others hadn't understood also. You were right with me, and the pianist and the conductor joined in.'

'Yes. But the rest of us wouldn't have understood in time.' He stopped the car outside Maree's coffee shop. 'I guess you won't do any resting till you see Maree. Just remember, you can't do any cleaning up.'

Maree saw them at the door and came quickly to open it, and she and Brooke hugged each other as well as Brooke's crutches permitted.

'I'm sorry, Maree. I'm sorry.'

'Sorry?' Maree smiled. 'It's no way your fault. And it's cleaned up, and people have been marvellous, lending me cups and plates and things. The girls who work here, and

159

Patricia and Harley, have all been working like Trojans. I'll be in business again this afternoon. The place was insured and the assessor was here early. I'm afraid insurance assessors are having a busy day in Broadfell,' she added soberly. 'The police have been, of course, and I guess they'll want to talk to you as well. So will quite a few other people, I think. We're just thankful you weren't terribly hurt.'

Tom took Brooke home and made her lunch and gave orders that she was to rest, but Maree's prediction was accurate. People came. Not only Patricia and Harley and Barry Endicott, the school principal, but several parents of children who had been in the choir, and several others phoned.

She thanked them all, and was touched to the point of tears, because she knew perfectly well that, whatever else, most of them still believed she was probably a murderer. They may not have forgiven her for that, but they believed her quick grasp of the danger may have saved their children.

The police came, also. The same two detectives, plus a third man who carried a suitcase and was introduced as Constable McClintock.

They all seated themselves and Sergeant Thorpe said, 'We're sorry to trouble you, Mrs

Hardwick, when I'm sure you don't feel particularly well after last night's accident in the storm, but it would appear very probable that the men who threatened an attack against Miss Stewart if you didn't give them the drugs they believed you had, have carried out their threat, at least in part.'

Brooke nodded. 'Unfortunately, yes. I'd begun to hope they believed me and would leave everyone alone. Did you get any leads from the vandalism last night?'

'One or two things that may be helpful. Our immediate concern is that these men will almost certainly contact you again very soon. They've shown you they will resort to violence against property. It's only a short step from there to violence against the person.'

Brooke gave a shiver. 'I didn't think you took their threats very seriously.'

'I assure you we are taking them very seriously now, since clearly they weren't empty talk. Having proved that, they will expect you to be sufficiently afraid for your friend's safety to co-operate with them. We want you to do just that.'

She stared at him. 'But — Sergeant, I can't tell them anything. I don't *know* anything. That's the absolute truth! For God's sake, can't I convince *anyone*?'

161

He held up a hand. 'Oddly enough, I believe you. But we would like you to help us catch these men before they resort to worse violence. Will you help?'

'Help? How?'

'I believe they'll phone you, and soon, rather than risk coming here. Constable McClintock is an expert on electronic surveillance. He will attach a bug to your phone and record whatever is said. That's an invasion of your privacy, if you like to say so. But to protect that privacy, although he will stay here with you and listen to incoming calls, he will record and try to trace only on a signal from you that this is the call we expect. Will you do this?'

'But when the demand comes, what then?'

'We want you to agree to give them the stuff. Tell them you don't have it here, but you'll get it. Then drive away somewhere — anywhere — or if you can't drive, Constable McClintock will drive you. He'll go with you in any case. Tell them you'll leave the package in a certain place. We'll keep watch on that place.'

She was silent for several moments. 'If I simply refuse to cooperate with these people, do you think they might actually harm Maree? To force my hand? You're not going to these lengths just to catch a couple of fellows who might be drug-addicts as well as vandals.'

The sergeant's expression didn't alter, but his tone was suddenly grim. 'I'm afraid harming Miss Stewart may very well be on their agenda. These are not nice people.'

Brooke nodded slowly. 'Tell me what you want me to do. Of course I'll do it.'

'Thank you. There's a small, green post-mounted rubbish-bin in the north-eastern corner of the park by the public swimming-pool. There's a picnic-table near it. Tell whoever phones that you'll put the package, wrapped in newspaper, in that bin. We'll be watching, but you won't see us. Then just drive home. On no account agree to meet these people.'

'That,' Brooke said with feeling, 'I can guarantee. Even with Constable McClintock around.'

'I think their phonecall will be brief, for fear we've put a trace on it. Don't try too obviously to keep them talking. We don't want them to get suspicious, and besides, the facilities these days will trace a call very quickly indeed, so that's not a problem. And, Mrs Hardwick, thanks. And good luck.'

He and Detective Hanson stood up to leave, while Constable McClintock was already busy with his electronics. Freckled, with cropped sandy hair and alert blue eyes, he looked barely more than a schoolboy, but clearly he knew precisely what he was doing.

Detective Hanson said to Brooke, 'I hear it's very fortunate for quite a few people that you were in the concert audience last night. How much are you hurt?'

'Only a cut leg and some bruises.' She smiled. 'I heal quickly.'

He smiled back. 'Good,' was all he said.

McClintock quickly finished attaching his gadgetry and cheerfully told Brooke not to pay him any attention when she had harmless calls. 'The moment you realize it's the extortionist, raise your hand and every syllable will go on tape. The hardest part for you will be waiting. We could have to wait a long time. The call might not come until this evening, but almost certainly they won't leave it any longer than that. In case they do decide to actually come to the house — and I think that's unlikely — don't open the door to anyone until you ask who it is. If it's them, tell them you have to put a dressing-gown on. That'll give me time to disappear with my toys into the next room.'

'What if they break in by picking a lock, like last time?'

He grinned. 'Well, then they'll get ever such a surprise.'

164

Something in the way he said it gave her considerable confidence in him.

The time, as he had predicted, dragged in nervous waiting. Tom called, and so did Harley, and Patricia, who said she would bring along a meal later, something that would only need to be heated in the microwave. Brooke tried to read. Tried to hold a conversation with Constable McClintock, who told her to call him Bill, but her mind kept wandering, waiting for the expected call, jumping every time the phone rang.

It was late afternoon before the call came.

'Now you know we're not bluffing,' a man's voice said without preamble, and she raised her hand to Bill McClintock, who had instantly flicked the switch on the recording device. 'Next time it won't be just cups and plates. So talk. Fast.'

Her heart hammering, Brooke said hoarsely, 'All right. I'll get the stuff for you.'

'Just tell us where it is.'

'No. I — can't. You mustn't know. I'll get it. Now, listen. There's a small, green litter-bin on a post in the north-east corner of the park by the swimming-pool. I'll wrap the package in newspaper and put it in that bin. I can have it there in an hour. I have — '

'Good God!' the man said, and there was

something near to panic in his voice. 'You were telling the truth! You don't know anything.'

He slammed the phone down.

In total bewilderment, Brooke slowly hung up and looked at Bill McClintock.

He listened a moment and then nodded. 'It was from a public pay phone at Mooloolaba,' he told her. 'You could hear the surf, so it was on the beach front. Smart cookie. He wasn't taking chances in case we had a trace on him. Long before anyone could get near the call-box, he'd have melted into the Sunday afternoon crowd in seconds — no hope of identifying him.'

He punched numbers on his mobile phone and reported the fiasco to Sergeant Thorpe.

Then he looked at Brooke, who was sitting huddled in her chair, trying to stop shaking. He went to her and put a hand on her shoulder.

'You've had a hell of a twenty-four hours,' he said gently. 'I'll make a cup of tea. The Sarge is coming to pick me up, but he'll be about fifteen minutes.'

The electronics expert proved adequately domesticated, and brought tea and some fruit-cake he had found by discreet rummaging in cupboards, and sat beside Brooke and talked easily to her — 'More,' she was later to tell Patricia, 'as though I was a normal human being instead of a murder-suspect simply being useful to inquiries.'

When the detectives came, Brooke looked at Sergeant Thorpe and spread her hands helplessly. 'I'm sorry. I just don't know what went wrong.'

They replayed the tape several times before the sergeant spoke. 'No need to apologize, Mrs Hardwick. You played your part perfectly. The false information I asked you to give simply didn't fit the picture. I had in mind a package of hard drugs, of maybe even up to a couple of kilograms. Obviously, whatever it is, it's much bigger. Evidently there's no way it would fit in a small garbage-bin. Maybe it's a half-tonne of hashish, disguised somewhere as — who knows? Potting-mix? Bales of hay? At least I think *you* can forget those unpleasant gentlemen, even if we can't. They know, now, that you don't know anything about the stuff they want.'

'You think he was convinced of that?'

'I'm certain. He was shocked, but that only proved he was convinced. And he didn't like knowing you couldn't help him no matter what he did.'

Brooke closed her eyes for a moment. 'Oh, God, I hope you're right. It would be marvellous to be able to forget them.'

Sergeant Thorpe was watching her with his usual intensity, but he smiled very faintly. 'Forgetting them mightn't come quickly, but I'm quite sure you can stop fearing them, both for yourself and your friend.'

'Will you tell her? She might be more convinced if she hears it from you.'

'We'll tell her. But if you'd feel better, by all means stay together for a few nights — Miss Stewart coming here might be best, since you're injured. It's an unnecessary precaution, I'm sure, but you may both feel better not being alone.'

He stood up and looked at the tape recorder. 'He believed you,' he said, almost to himself. 'But he was very worried. And I would love to know why.'

7

The sergeant was evidently right. There were no further threats from menacing strangers.

Although she was to some degree buoyed up by anger, Maree was shaken at first by the vandalism of her coffee shop, but she set enthusiastically to work, getting it back to normal. Her loyal staff of two gave her full support, and Harley always seemed to be there when she needed him. Under his easygoing manner there was a warmth and a kindness Brooke had always known, and Maree discovered.

It gave Brooke no surprise, but great delight, when Maree and Harley came to see her one evening and Maree, eyes dancing, said, 'Brooke, would you approve of me as a cousin-in-law, if there's such a thing? We're getting married.'

Brooke laughed and hugged them both. 'I approve.'

Broadfell repaired the storm-damaged buildings, cleared away the wreckage of trees, replanted smashed gardens, mourned the life lost, was thankful for the lives saved, and no longer knew quite what to think or how to

169

feel about Brooke Hardwick, murder-suspect.

For Brooke, the attempts to drive her out of business ceased, and life resumed some kind of normality, though she could never forget for more than a fleeting moment that, although the town might look at her more kindly, suspicions were not possible to discard, even for the kindliest. And for the police nothing had changed.

She had the call from Damien's mother before she left for work.

When the phone rang on that bright, early-summer morning which held a suggestion that sapping heat might not be far away, she picked it up without trepidation.

Rachel Hardwick's voice, crisp and decisive and brooking no argument, said without preamble, 'I want to see you, Brooke. Today.'

'Rachel!'

Rachel never phoned for a chat. Rachel, in fact, never phoned and never chatted, at least not to Brooke.

'I'm just on my way to work,' Brooke said pleasantly. 'I'm afraid I'm pretty busy this week. What about the weekend?'

'Today,' Rachel said flatly. 'You can think about the future. I can't. I need to see you. Today. I'm in Wesley Hospital.' She gave a room number.

'In hospital! I'm sorry, I didn't know . . . '

She stopped. Rachel Hardwick had hung up. Brooke put the handset down slowly.

You can think about the future. I can't.

Rachel was not given to dramatization. Quite the reverse. A display of any kind of emotion was totally scorned. Rachel had just told her she was dying, and apparently it would be soon. Death would be something she would accept as stone-facedly as she had accepted her son's marriage to a woman she considered totally inappropriate. Doubtless she would have fought death just as she had opposed Damien's marriage, but once it was clear that the battle was lost she would abdicate with the same cold dignity.

The last thing she would want from Brooke was sympathy. The last thing she would want to offer was a last-minute reconciliation.

Yet she had said, 'I need to see you. Today.' It had not been a plea, but a command. Nevertheless, Brooke thought, there had been a very real *need* behind that imperious order.

She picked up the phone again and called the landscaping office. Dean's voice answered cheerfully, and as cheerfully told her that sure, Mrs H., he could handle everything today.

'I'll probably be back this afternoon probably by lunch time. My mother-in-law is very ill in Brisbane and wants to see me. Thanks, Dean.'

In spite of what Rachel had said, Brooke was shocked at the change in her mother-in-law's appearance. In the few months since Damien's funeral, his mother, always slightly built, had shrunk to almost unrecognizable gauntness. The hands that rested on the bedclothes were almost skeletal, veins like blue cords under white, semi-translucent skin. But the grey hair against the pillows was impeccably groomed, and the sunken eyes had lost none of their intense alertness.

'So you did come,' she greeted Brooke tersely, the voice, though clear, betraying the obviously hated weakness of the body.

'I'm sorry you're so ill,' Brooke said. She put one hand gently over one of Rachel's, but the hand under hers made no reciprocal movement of greeting.

'Sit down,' Rachel said. 'I have things to say.'

Brooke obediently drew up a chair.

'No doubt,' her mother-in-law said without inflection, 'you're surprised I wanted to see you.'

'Somewhat,' Brooke agreed with a smile of total non-antagonism. 'You never liked me.'

Rachel seemed to think about it. 'No. But possibly only in the context of being

Damien's wife. I told him he was making a mistake, but he made his choice. I never *disliked* you. You were wrong for Damien, that's all.'

Brooke knew that was as close to a reconciliation as Rachel would ever get, so she simply nodded.

'Damien,' Rachel said, 'should never have married anyone, least of all someone like you. He never told you about Allison, did he?'

Puzzled, Brooke shook her head.

'He was an engineering student when he met her. He was going to be a civil engineer, not a minister. Did you know that?'

Brooke nodded. 'Yes. I knew that.'

'Well, Allison was another student. He was madly in love with her. She was a charming girl, tall, fair — and addicted to heroin. They lived together for about six months, and Damien tried to get her off the drugs. He thought he'd succeeded. Then one day he came home and found her dead from a heroin overdose. She had a bottle of sleeping-tablets in the bathroom cabinet. He couldn't face living without her. He took the lot.'

She paused and reached for the glass of water beside her, impatiently waving away Brooke's move to help.

'He was found in a coma, and they saved

his life with great difficulty. But something in him was changed forever. When he recovered, he said God had called him to do His work, so he left engineering for theology. It wasn't just religion that was the change in him. There was something else, some damage to the brain, I suppose, as a result of the overdose-induced coma. Only a strong woman could ever have hoped to cope with being Damien's wife after that. You weren't right. You might have been all right before, but never after he changed. You were a poor stick who just tried to please him. You never understood how to handle him.'

Shocked, Brooke was staring at her. 'Why didn't you tell me this long ago?'

Rachel moved a hand in a brief gesture of impatience. 'It wouldn't have done the least good. You'd just have been soft and sympathetic. That would have been no good at all.'

She looked squarely at Brooke, her eyes suddenly tired looking, the fierce brightness faded. 'I should think,' she said unexpectedly, 'he made you very unhappy. They do, these people who believe they're directed by God.'

Brooke could think of nothing to say for a moment. Then she said quietly, 'I didn't kill him.'

A ghost of a smile flickered across Rachel's

face. 'No,' she said. 'I never supposed you did. Go now. I've told you, and I'm tired.'

She sank back in clear exhaustion, her eyes closed, her frail body scarcely more than a tiny hump under the bedclothes.

The dismissal was final, and Brooke knew no gesture of sympathy or attempted friendship was wanted. 'Thank you for telling me, Rachel,' she said as she stood up to leave. 'I wish things had been different.'

As she reached the door, Rachel said, 'Brooke.'

Brooke turned. The older woman's eyes were open again, fixed on her with a new intensity.

'He had strange dreams which weren't ever going to come true. Sometimes dreams are dangerous. It is better that he never knew those dreams for what they were. It is better. Remember that.'

The eyes closed again, the face against the pillow looked even more gaunt, as if the effort of talking had totally drained the ailing body that held the intense brain prisoner in its frailty.

Brooke said softly, 'Goodbye, Rachel.'

There was no acknowledgement.

Shaken more than she would have believed by the interview, Brooke found a place to have coffee and try to gather her thoughts together before she began the drive back to Broadfell.

She was still unsure exactly why Rachel had wanted to see her. To apologize — almost — for her son? No. But certainly to explain him. The thing which baffled Brooke was why?

Why had Rachel, after the years of total indifference, wanted Brooke to understand to some extent the reason for Damien's strange behaviour? In spite of what she had said, did she in fact think Brooke had murdered Damien, and she wanted to say obliquely that she understood? No, Brooke decided. If Rachel had thought her son's wife had killed him, she would have said so. Loud and clear and at once.

She sighed, and tried to concentrate on the drive home and, for the rest of the afternoon, on preparing the final tender for the landscaping at Blue Crystal Waters development.

By three o'clock she knew her mind wasn't on what she was doing, and she couldn't afford to make errors in calculations on a project of this importance. She sat for a few minutes, thinking of the dying woman she had spoken with — almost certainly for the last time — a few hours before. The body so frail, the mind and spirit so strong.

Suddenly she remembered, with a touch of guilt, that it was at least a fortnight since she had visited old Stewart Martin in the nursing home. A widower with no family, he had often come to church services before a series of strokes gradually robbed him of the strength of both mind and body, and forced him to give up his rather isolated farm and be placed in permanent care.

She knew that Damien had visited him regularly, and had been his only visitor, the nursing staff said — regretfully, as he was a great favourite with everyone. After Damien's death Brooke had taken to visiting the kindly, gentle old man, doing little errands for him if he wanted things like toiletries or new pyjamas, often taking him little treats such as ice-cream or chocolates. The nursing home was a half-hour drive from Broadfell, though, and over the past few weeks she had not visited the old man, who was such a mental contrast to Rachel Hardwick.

Brooke glanced at her watch, put plans and sketches and calculations and lists of shrubs away, locked the office, went into Broadfell village to buy chocolates, and then drove to the nursing home.

Stewart Martin was sitting in a wheelchair by the window, reading the same book he'd been reading the last three times she'd visited him.

'Hello, Mr Martin,' she said brightly. 'Good book?'

He looked up blankly, and then recognition dawned. 'Sure is a good book,' he declared.

The nurses had told Brooke that he would read it right through to the end, put it aside, and pick it up again the next day and start all over again, with no recollection of ever having read it before. But now he looked at Brooke sharply.

'Did you bring my rose?'

Brooke was startled. Last time she had visited him he had asked her if she would go out to the farm and bring him a rose 'from the bush by the gate.' She had believed he would have forgotten about it before she had gone as far as the nursing home's front door. Now, three weeks or more on, it was uppermost in his mind.

'I'm so sorry, Mr Martin,' she said. 'I've been awfully busy. I'll go out on Saturday, if you like.'

He nodded. 'You're a good girl. That preacher husband of yours is lucky. You bring me one of them roses down by the front gate. Two-coloured, they are, never seen any others like 'em, meself. Wife planted that bush. If I get one of them roses it'll buck me up so much I'll be out of here in a day or so, you'll see.'

Brooke smiled in spite of the little twist of sadness inside her, because only death would let Stewart Martin leave the nursing home.

'I'll get the rose for you,' she said. 'I promise. If the bush isn't in flower right now I'll keep going back till it is.'

★ ★ ★

She had asked Patricia and Cameron and Maree to have dinner with her at the cottage that evening, Harley having had to go to Brisbane to attend a pharmacists' conference, and she told them about Stewart and his rose.

'I've never actually been out to his farm,' she said. 'I believe it's fairly isolated. I think I'll see if I can buy a bicoloured rose from the flower-shop.'

'You probably could,' Patricia said, 'but if this old gentleman is fully alert sometimes, it just might be one of his lucid moments, and there are lots of two-toned roses. You might get it all wrong.'

'Oh.' Brooke sighed. 'Yes, I might. And that might really upset him, to think that I'd tried to cheat and not bothered to get him the one thing he really wants. I'll go out there on

Saturday. I hope the wretched bush is still alive.'

'Can I go, Brooke?' Cameron asked. 'Are there cows and things? Can Chips come?' Chips was his dog.

'Oh, Cameron,' Patricia said. 'Brooke mightn't want a small boy chattering in her ear, let alone a large dog in her car.'

'Mum!' Cameron made a show of looking pained. 'I hold an intelligent conversation. I don't *chatter*. And Chips is awfully well behaved and he'd love to go to a farm. I wouldn't let him chase anything.'

Brooke laughed. 'All right, you talked me into it. I tell you what, why don't we all go? You can both leave your off-siders to look after things for you for an hour, can't you? Unless you and Harley have plans, Maree?'

'Dinner, but he's playing tennis in the afternoon.'

'Right. Neither of you takes much time off, so it'd do you good, and I can have protection from any bogy-men who might be hanging around a deserted farm.'

'Is it really deserted?' Cameron eagerly wanted to know. 'Like an empty house and everything?'

Brooke smiled. 'It's deserted all right, but there's no house. Probably a shed or two, I suppose, but I don't know.'

'Why isn't there a house?' Cameron demanded. 'Mr Martin must've lived in a house. We could pretend it's haunted and real scary.'

'Well, you might have to settle for a haunted milking-shed. The house was burned down.'

'Golly! What happened?'

'The poor old gentleman had been having a series of little strokes which made him so forgetful he really shouldn't have been living alone. He'd given up dairy-farming and leased his farmland to a neighbouring farmer, but he wouldn't sell the property or leave it.'

'Why wouldn't he, if he was sick?' Cameron asked.

'He wanted to stay because it was his home,' Brooke said.

'Then one day he turned on an electric heater without noticing he'd put the newspaper, or something like that, on it, and he went out for a walk and never saw his house was on fire. Neighbours next door saw smoke — they couldn't see the house itself from their place — and drove over and called the fire brigade, but of course there was nothing anyone could do. Mr Martin suffered shock, naturally, which was probably the cause of a more severe stroke, and he had to go into a nursing home. He doesn't remember the fire, and he

181

doesn't know the farm's deserted. He thinks he'll be home in a day or two, working the farm.'

'Poor man,' Patricia said softly. 'Well, then, let's all go out and get his rose. I hope we can get him an armful of them, if the bush survived the fire.'

★   ★   ★

The private road into the farm was a simple gravel track, still not badly rutted by rain, but reduced to no more than two wheel-tracks with grass growing enthusiastically between, running for about four hundred metres, between tree-dotted pastures and low hills which hid the farm-buildings from neighbouring houses and the public road. Cattle — sleek black and white Friesians — grazed behind well-kept fences, evidently maintained by the neighbouring farmer who leased Stewart Martin's property. A sturdy weldmesh gate hung squarely across the farm-track between concrete posts.

'What's the betting it's locked?' Brooke said glumly. 'Still, I suppose we can climb through the fence. I hope there isn't an irate bull on the other side, that's all.'

The gate, however, was simply latched, and Cameron opened it and they drove through.

182

The area around the sheds and the site where the house had been was fenced off from the rest of the farm, doubtless acceding to Mr Martin's wish to 'leave things alone', and clearly no cattle — irate bull or otherwise — grazed there. Grass grew rank everywhere, except for some parts of the blackened earth where the fire had reduced an old man's dreams to rubble. Someone had cleared all the rubble away long ago, leaving only a rectangle of concrete which looked as if it might have been the floor of a downstairs laundry and garage.

The milking-shed still stood, weeds and grass pushing up through cracks in the concrete flooring. All the machinery was gone, the timber rails of the holding-yards sagging drunkenly here and there. A large shed, probably serving as a barn or machinery shed, stood off to one side, its big double doors padlocked shut in the only sign of anything but total, uncaring neglect.

'What a shame,' Maree said. 'It looks as if it was cared for once — pride taken in it.'

'Poor Mr Martin,' Brooke said. 'I'm glad he can't see it.'

Patricia was watching Cameron, who was happily exploring, his dog at his heels. 'Cameron may not find them,' she said quietly, 'but there are ghosts of a kind here, all right. The ghosts of a family's dreams. Think of all the years of activity, of work, worry, laughter, tears. And now this. It's much more than change. It's — emptiness.'

She turned to Brooke. 'Didn't they have any family?'

Brooke shook her head. 'No. That's why there was no one to take charge of his affairs when Mr Martin became unable to properly fend for himself.'

Patricia looked puzzled. 'How long has he been in the nursing home?'

'Oh, a couple of years, I suppose, maybe more. Of course, he had to give up dairying before then, but he wouldn't dream of leaving the place. He and his wife had come here when they were first married, he told us.'

Patricia nodded. 'I was mistaken, then. When you spoke yesterday about coming out here I thought he must be the man Damien bought some fertilizer for, just before he was killed. He said it was for a farmer who was in hospital and had asked Damien to get the fertilizer for him so it would be there ready for him to spread as soon as he got home. I didn't have much of the right sort, because mostly I just keep organic stuff. When you mentioned Mr Martin being in the nursing home I thought that was the name of the man Damien had bought the fertilizer for. But obviously it wasn't — or it was another Martin. It's a long time since Mr Martin did any farming. I wonder if there's any chance his wife's rose is still surviving?'

'It might be,' Maree said. 'Roses are pretty hardy. It depends how close it was to the house, I guess. If it was close, probably the fire would have destroyed it. But there are still a few shrubs growing there where the garden once was.'

Some of the fence which had enclosed the house and garden was still standing, but the garden was largely lost under weeds and grass.

'He said it was near the gate,' Brooke said.

A wooden gate hung on one hinge, and a weed-encrusted paved path still showed the way to where the front of the house had stood. A rose bush grew on either side, one with two white blossoms showing above clambering weeds, the other carrying one bud and one fully open bloom with a deep cream centre shading to rich pink on the outer edges of the petals.

Brooke smiled with delight. 'It's done the right thing for him! And it is a lovely rose.'

'Peer Gynt, I think,' Patricia said. 'It's not going to give in to weeds and general neglect, either.'

She and Maree bent down and began

tugging weeds and grass away from both bushes, while Brooke produced secateurs from the pocket of her jeans and carefully cut the rose with a long stem. They all worked for a little while and succeeded in clearing most of the choking weeds away.

Presently Patricia said wryly, 'I don't know quite why we're doing this. In a few weeks the rubbish will all grow back again.'

'I suppose it's partly because the roses are putting up a fight against the odds,' Maree suggested. 'It always makes you want to help the underdog. But I guess that's about all we can do.'

They went out and pulled the sagging gate closed behind them. Brooke smiled to herself at the futility of the automatic gesture — futile because sections of the fence were missing anyway. But somehow it made her feel less of an intruder by not adding to the general neglect.

Cameron and Chips came scampering across to them. 'Do we have to go now? I haven't finished exploring.'

His mother laughed. 'You'd spend all day at it, I'm sure. But yes, we do have to go.'

'Mr Martin was lucky he didn't lose his car when the house got burned,' Cameron said.

'Oh, but he did, I'm afraid,' Brooke told him. 'It was in a garage that was attached to the house, I remember hearing, and it went, along with everything else. It was a Toyota Hilux utility pick-up, I remember, because he used to drive it to church.'

'Well, he must've had two cars,' Cameron said, 'because there's a van in the big shed.'

'You haven't been poking about in there, have you?' his mother asked anxiously. 'Because it's all closed up, and you shouldn't go in anywhere that's closed up.'

'Stop worrying, Mum. I didn't go in. It's locked, anyway.'

'Are you sure there's a van in there?' Brooke queried. 'How can you tell?'

'Well, the shed's pretty old, and there are sort of spaces between the boards, and I looked in. Come and see for yourself.'

They all dutifully trooped over to the big shed and peered through spaces between warped weather-boards. There was a wheel-barrow and a small pile of empty stock-meal sacks, and there was indeed a white, one-ton van, certainly far from new, but not derelict, either.

'Well, it hasn't been standing there for the past two years,' Brooke said. 'It'd be covered in dust and cobwebs. The neighbour who rents the farm must keep it here for some reason.'

Cameron's eyes gleamed. 'It might belong to a gang of international jewel thieves, or bank robbers. That could be it. It's the bank robbers' getaway vehicle and they've hidden it here with all the loot till the heat's off.'

They all laughed. 'Well,' Brooke said cheerfully, 'that would be more interesting than simply belonging to a neighbour. We'd better get out of here before we get arrested as accessories to the crime. And before Mr Martin's rose wilts.'

'Can we come again?' Cameron wanted to know. 'This place is fun.'

'Only if Mr Martin asks me to come,' Brooke said.

'He might want another rose, mightn't he?'

'If he does, you can come too,' Brooke told him, 'to protect me from the bank robbers.'

Cameron grinned. 'I don't expect it really does belong to bank robbers. But the next-door farmer won't mind if I *pretend* it does, will he? It's more fun than just thinking it's full of cow-feed or something, isn't it?'

'Much more,' Brooke agreed.

'I hope,' Patricia said, 'that poor Mr Martin hasn't forgotten all about his rose when you take it to him.'

Stewart Martin, though, had not forgotten his rose, and his transparent delight in it gave Brooke's spirits a lift that kept her smiling all the way home.

Then the smile froze. A police car was standing outside.

8

She shivered as if someone had flung a bucket of iced water over her. Police did not come to see you on a Saturday afternoon, late, on a routine inquiry.

Nauseated, forcing herself to move calmly, she put the car in the garage, locked the door, and walked to the front door, where the two detectives she had come to know much better than she would have chosen, having eased themselves out of the car where they had been sitting, were waiting for her.

'Good-afternoon, Mrs Hardwick,' the sergeant said. He looked suitably solemn for someone about to make an arrest, Brooke thought bitterly; Detective Hanson, on the other hand, was smilingly cheerful. Mission accomplished.

'May we come in?' Sergeant Thorpe asked politely. 'We need to talk.'

Brooke, her hands shaking so that she could barely fit the key into the lock of the front door, scarcely heard him. David Hanson wordlessly took the key from her, unlocked the door and gestured for her to go in.

As they walked into the neat little

sitting-room the sergeant said, 'You've heard nothing more from the men who broke into your house — the ones you call the balaclavas — and who presumably vandalized Miss Stewart's premises?'

'No.' She looked at him closely. 'Have you had any success in identifying them? I thought, anyway, that you were sure they realized I couldn't tell them what they wanted to know.'

'I am confident of that. But one can't ever be entirely sure they won't try once more. And no, unfortunately, we're no closer to identifying them.'

She sat down wearily, gripped her hands tightly together and looked squarely at Harold Thorpe. 'That's not why you came, is it?'

'No.' He took some sheets of folded paper from an inside coat-pocket. 'Do you mind if we sit down?'

Brooke gestured to the other chairs in the room and the two men sat down.

'Mrs Hardwick,' the sergeant said quietly, 'we have some very strange news which may come as a considerable shock to you. Did you have a close relationship with your husband's mother?'

She shook her head, bewildered. 'No, Sergeant. Rachel always considered me to be totally unsuited to be Damien's wife.' A twitch of a rueful smile touched her mouth. 'As it turned out, she was no doubt correct.'

'I see. And your feelings towards her?'

Brooke shrugged. 'I truly never knew her much. From my viewpoint she was neither friend nor foe. I regretted her rejection of me. I lost my parents a considerable time ago, and Rachel's friendship would have been valued. But she didn't wish it.'

She looked from one to the other of the detectives with sharpened alertness. 'Why are you asking me this?'

'Mrs Hardwick, I have to tell you that Mrs Rachel Hardwick died early on Thursday morning.'

'Died!' She stared at him. 'But — I saw her on Wednesday morning. She — oh, my Lord.' Brooke shook her head as if to clear it. 'She phoned me that morning — Wednesday — and insisted I should go to see her in the hospital that day. I asked if it couldn't wait till the weekend, and she said no, that I had time, she didn't. I realized when I saw her that she was dying — I hadn't known she was ill — but I never guessed it would be so soon. She must have known.'

'Yes. The hospital didn't notify you because Mrs Hardwick had given specific instructions that only her solicitor was to be told when she died. She also gave specific instructions to her solicitor. One of those instructions was that there was to be no formal funeral, just a strictly private, very brief service in the crematorium chapel, which she had already arranged, with only the solicitor and one member of his staff in attendance. The service was held yesterday.'

Brooke shook her head, baffled. 'But why? Even if Rachel didn't want me there, she must have had friends.'

The sergeant nodded. 'Probably. But she left her solicitor a letter, given to him a little time ago apparently, to be opened and acted upon only in the event of her death.'

He unfolded a sheet of handwritten paper. 'The solicitor had this delivered to us by special courier yesterday — again as his client had directed.' He held the paper out to Brooke. 'I'm afraid it will give you a considerable shock.'

Brooke took the paper. Rachel's small, precise, distinctive handwriting covered a sheet of quality writing-paper. It was headed: 'To be read and delivered to the appropriate authorities, in accordance with the attached instructions, on the occasion of my death.'

The rest of the document read: 'I am fully aware that I have very little time left to live. I am selfish enough to wish to live that time without the abysmal difficulties this information would cause. I regret that suspicion for the murder of my son, Damien Hardwick, has fallen on his wife, but I was always aware that this suspicion would not last very long — not longer than my remaining life.

'I loved my son. There had always been complete trust between us, which doubtless is why he told me of the evil thing he planned to do. He told me that he had manufactured suspicion that Brooke, his wife, was using hard drugs. He said that this was in case suspicion should fall on him, even though he felt that this could not happen. But, he said, if it did, if he was by any chance implicated, people would believe they understood why he felt compelled to act.

'I could not allow him to do what he planned. I could forgive my son, perhaps, but not allow him to commit such a monstrous evil. I drove to Broadfell and parked my car in a side-street, and went to the house. There was music playing. The front door was unlocked, so I simply walked in. I knew Brooke was out. I knew where Damien kept his shot-gun. I took it out, loaded it, and walked to the study door. He was sitting at his desk and hadn't heard me. I could have killed him without him ever knowing who it was, but I felt he should know why he had to die, so I spoke to him, and told him. He began to walk toward me. He said I didn't understand. But I did. I understood exactly.

'I killed my only child. He, of course, was no longer normal. There is nothing on earth more dangerous than someone who believes he is directed by God to do violence. I had and will have for all the life that remains to me, the most profound sadness. But no regret. It had to be done. I did it. May God forgive us both. Rachel Hardwick.'

★ ★ ★

Brooke read the paper a second time, unable to grasp its contents in one stunned reading. Then she raised shocked eyes to the sergeant's face.

'Rachel!' she said, her voice barely above a whisper. '*Rachel*? But — why? Was there anything — another letter — anything — to say why? What was it that he planned that would drive Rachel — *Rachel* — to kill him?'

'There was no explanation,' Sergeant Thorpe said, his tone surprisingly gentle. 'But our handwriting and forensic people who examined your husband's personal diary, confirmed what Detective Hanson had immediately suspected: the entries were faked. That is, they had all been written at the

194

same time. The diary was not a chronological record at all. A psychologist who read the diary said it clearly had been designed to implicate you in drug use, and he expressed the opinion that it suggested your husband may have been planning to murder you by means of a drug overdose made to look like an accident. That, of course, is only supposition.'

He glanced from Brooke's white-faced shock to David Hanson. 'David, make Mrs Hardwick a cup of tea, would you? Lots of sugar in it.'

'I don't take . . . ' Brooke began mechanically.

Sergeant Thorpe cut in with a smile, 'This time you need it.'

He said nothing else, and Brooke sat silently, the sheet of paper in her hand, reading it again and again, trying to comprehend the incomprehensible. Presently the sergeant held out his hand and she gave him the paper.

He nodded. 'Thank you. There will be a further coroner's hearing into your husband's death, and naturally this is vital evidence which will make the inquest only a formality. To safe-guard your interests, we have had several photocopies made of this original.' He handed her two clear copies. 'I suggest you give one to your solicitor and keep one yourself. Naturally, this removes any hint of suspicion from you and leaves your innocence beyond question.'

Brooke put the papers in the drawer of a small side-table, brain whirling, movements mechanical. Then she turned and stared at Sergeant Thorpe.

'You knew — you had this information yesterday. And you did nothing! You didn't even bother to *tell* me! Do you have any idea — any faint glimmer of an idea — what it's like to be suspected of a murder you knew nothing about until you walked into your home and found the body?'

Fury flamed in her eyes and shook her voice. 'You did nothing! You've let me go on for twenty-four hours more than I need have, suffering this ghastly awareness of suspicion — not just from you. From people who were my friends. And it didn't even *matter* to you! Can't you *see*?'

He stood up quickly. 'Mrs Hardwick, listen to me. I am sorry. You can believe that or not as you choose. But I am not unaware of the fact that you've been in an extremely unhappy situation.'

'Then why didn't you tell me about this letter yesterday? Or didn't you think another day would make any difference?'

'Look, I can well understand you're

angry. But although this document, and all the other information from Mrs Rachel Hardwick's solicitor, came into our hands yesterday, we had to have this confession verified by our experts as being genuine. We only received that information this afternoon.'

Brooke stared at him for a few seconds and then nodded. 'Yes. I see. I'm sorry.'

She sat down again and so did the sergeant, just as Detective Hanson brought in a mug of hot, black tea and handed it to her. She sipped the sickly sweet drink and found it oddly comforting. She was shivering with shock, but the hot sweetness gradually helped to subdue the shakes. The detectives watched her closely, but said nothing.

Presently she said slowly, 'Rachel never liked me. Yet if you're right, she killed the son she adored, in order to save my life. That's an awesome thing to have to live with for the rest of my life.'

Detective Hanson said gravely, 'Perhaps she saw it as saving her son as well. She couldn't bear to think of him as a convicted murderer. Don't let it weigh on you, Mrs Hardwick. To me, that letter indicates her concern for her son was uppermost. She believed he was better dead.'

'Perhaps.' Brooke looked from one policeman to the other. 'But why did Damien plan to kill me? When I wanted to leave him, he stopped me with threats. But if I'd left him, he could forever have played the injured party, and had everyone's sympathy. And he'd have been free of me, if that's what he wanted, with absolutely no risk to himself. Why try to *kill* me?'

'As to that,' Sergeant Thorpe said, 'we have no more idea than you have. Remember that Rachel Hardwick wrote that her son was no longer normal. Do you feel that was correct?'

'Yes.' She nodded. 'His behaviour was full of contradictions. But even an unbalanced mind must have a reason to want to kill someone — even if that reason makes no sense to anyone else. Why didn't I understand what he was planning? There was only ever one brief moment when I was physically afraid of him, and then I told myself I'd imagined it.'

The sergeant said, 'People with dangerously disturbed minds seldom give a hint of what they're thinking.'

'Except,' Brooke said slowly, 'in this case, Damien told his mother. And she prevented it.'

'Yes. But I agree with Detective Hanson: she did it, not really to shield you, but to protect her son from the consequences of his plans. Don't let it be a burden on you.'

'No. I suppose not.' She managed some semblance of a smile. 'Thank you.'

The detectives stood up. 'Mrs Hardwick,' David Hanson said, 'I think you should have a friend with you. You've had a pretty severe shock. A series of them lately, I'm afraid. Can I phone someone? Miss Stewart?'

'I'll be all right. I think I need to be alone for a few minutes to let this register with me. I'll call a few special friends presently.'

She smiled, and this time it was a smile that lit her eyes. 'I guess it takes a few minutes to adjust to freedom, and that's rather like what this is like. Or like walking from a cold darkness into sunlight. Just for a moment I want to savour it by myself, in case it turns out to be only a dream.'

Sergeant Thorpe said quietly, 'It may surprise you to know that Detective Hanson and I are both glad for you. Even policemen are human. We've released a simple statement to the media. I suspect they have largely lost interest, but the nature of the whole thing will recreate some interest in it, and it may mean some reporters will arrive on your doorstep. At least if anyone harboured any suspicions of you, those suspicions will be put to rest.'

When they had gone, she sat for a long

time, trying to come to terms with what had happened. Sat, filled with a profound regret that someone with Rachel Hardwick's incredible strength of character should have been placed in the hideous position of feeling compelled to do what she had done.

Finally Brooke stood up and took a long, deep breath. 'It's over,' she said aloud. 'I can begin to pick myself up and go back to normal living. The nightmare's over.'

She couldn't know that it was not.

9

Later that evening she sat with Tom, Maree and Harley and Patricia, having asked them all to come as a thing of urgency, and she told them and showed them the photocopies of Rachel's letter. They hugged her joyfully, and sat soberly, reflecting, as Brooke had done, on the agony of spirit Damien's mother had endured.

'Nevertheless,' Tom said, 'she let you go through God only knows what torment, suspected for all these months as you have been.'

Brooke shrugged. 'Maybe if she did it to save my life, she thought it wasn't much of a price for me to pay.'

'Do you think she did it to save your life?' Harley asked. 'Or to save her precious son from the consequences of committing murder? Consequences she evidently regarded as a fate worse than death.'

It was a question for which Brooke had no answer, then or later, when, as Harold Thorpe had predicted, the media arrived on her doorstep, in numbers which surprised her.

'Don't knock it,' Harley advised her with

the lazy grin that hid his genuine caring. 'You've had to stand up under all the suspicion that's been heaped on you. Grab the chance to throw it off and let everyone know the truth.'

The news was duly spread by the media that 'in a bizarre twist' the shot-gun murder of the Reverend Damien Hardwick in Broadfell some months ago had been solved, his recently-deceased mother having left a sealed confession with her solicitor.

A statement released by police said that Mrs Rachel Hardwick had confessed to killing her son, whom she believed to have become deranged, to prevent him from committing a crime of violence, the nature of which she had not specified, but which police believed to have been the planned murder of his wife.

When the news was spread, a number of local people who had remained friendly or non-committal, hastened to express their happiness at Brooke's exoneration. Those who had openly snubbed her clearly found it embarrassingly difficult. None hastened to apologize, and when they met her they treated her with some degree of awkwardness, but she had no doubt they would gradually revert to treating her just as they had before Damien was killed.

She confessed to Tom that it was rather as if she had been away for a very long time, and everyone, herself included, had to readjust to the fact that she was home again.

But the sky seemed bluer, the clouds whiter, the bird-songs clearer, the summer heat far less tiring, and work, free now of threats, was a joy again. She was whistling a cheerful tune to herself as she went into Patricia's nursery on the Tuesday a week after the shackles of suspicion had been removed, and almost bumped into two men who were just leaving, clipboards and brief-cases in hand, white shirts, ties, trendy dark glasses. They smiled at her infectious gaiety and stepped aside to let her pass.

'They looked very government-department-on-official-business,' she said to Patricia cheerfully. 'Have you been importing prohibited plant-material or something equally fearsome?'

Patricia laughed. 'You sound happy, Brooke. It's great — really wonderful. And no, I haven't done anything illegal, and yes, they were Department of Primary Industry fellows doing a survey on nursery sales, for goodness sake. I often wonder just what these endless surveys really achieve.'

Brooke made a face. 'I know. I was kept on the phone for ten minutes the other day by someone doing a survey on just about everything from what brand of toothpaste I use to which party I'd vote for if there was an election next week.'

Jessica Woods, one of Patricia's assistants, paused in trundling a barrow of azaleas past. 'One of the TV stations has been doing a survey of people's opinions on that American fellow who's out here advocating free drugs for addicts. They're going to show the clips tonight.'

She smiled a shade grimly. 'That one should be a bit more interesting than government department stuff. I wonder how many people will agree with him?'

'Oh that Doctor — Crawley — Cawley, is it?' Patricia said. 'Mmm. I'm not sure how I'd answer if I was asked whether or not I agreed with him. On the face of it, handing out free heroin sounds plain insanity. But I know he argues that it would destroy the massive crime kingdoms that grow rich on people's misery.'

'Well, we're not winning the war by law-enforcement,' Jessica said. 'Drug use just keeps increasing. It always will, while ever it pays people handsomely to push it. The dealers set the price, and the poor fools who get themselves hooked will do anything to get the money. I'd say give them the stuff if they're dumb enough to use it. If they want to kill themselves with it — fine with me. As long as they don't go around killing other people to get the money.'

'Ye-es,' Brooke said a shade doubtfully. 'I'm not sure there's any simple solution, though.'

'It's worth thinking about, just the same, isn't it?' Jessica said. There was a passionate intensity about her that was in stark contrast to her normal happy-go-lucky manner.

'It certainly is,' Brooke agreed. 'And I think we need people like this American doctor to shake up our minds sometimes so we don't close the door on different ideas. But golly-whizz, it's too nice a morning to be fretting over the woes of the world. And I've got work to do and I'd better get on with it.'

Jessica smiled, the laughter-spark back in her eyes. 'I guess it'd look like a good morning to you if it was pouring rain, Mrs Hardwick. It must be great to have your name cleared. Dad and I are so glad for you.'

Brooke, touched by the clear sincerity, said, 'Thanks, Jessica. Thank you.'

When the girl went on out to the back of the nursery Brooke said with a little frown, 'She's very intense about drugs — more so than you'd expect from the average teenager.'

'Her mother was murdered by a drug-addict,' Patricia said quietly. 'A young man who broke into the house, looking for money to support his habit. Jessica's mother came home from shopping while he was still in the house.'

'Oh, dear God,' Brooke said, shocked. 'I'd no idea.'

'No. Well, you couldn't know. It's a good many years ago now. And don't let it spoil your day.' Patricia smiled at her. 'You deserve a lot of good days. And Barnaby and Jessica long ago picked themselves up and got on with their lives, even though there'll always be a bitterness about drugs lurking in their minds, and an emptiness in their lives.'

★   ★   ★

When Brooke got home that evening, Dianne Paton was waiting in her car by the front gate. Brooke hadn't seen her since the night of the storm, when Colin Paton had died under the falling tree. Brooke had written Dianne a brief note simply expressing sympathy and saying that Colin had lost his life in a very courageous act. She hadn't attended the funeral because the sight of someone Colin had found himself detesting, might have proved anything but consoling to his widow.

Now she looked at her visitor in frank

surprise. 'Dianne! It's good to see you. Will you come in?'

'Thank you.' Dianne Paton followed her into the house and sat on the edge of the chair Brooke indicated, as if poised for flight. The ravages of too recent grief and shock showed in the pale, hollow cheeks, the dark circles under the eyes that spoke of long, sleepless hours. Brooke waited quietly.

'Brooke, if Colin were alive I know he would come to apologize, for what little that's worth. I've come instead, as he'd want me to. We did you a cruel injustice.'

She held up a restraining hand as Brooke made to speak. 'We rushed to judgement and reached a terribly wrong conclusion.'

Brooke smiled wryly. 'So did half the village. It's all right, Dianne. I understand it.'

'That doesn't excuse it, especially not in us. We should have known you better. Colin thought so highly of Damien. He believed implicitly everything Damien said. I wasn't very much better. But there's something else I have to tell you. There — wouldn't have been any more vandalism attacks on people who did business with you — even if the truth about what happened to Damien hadn't come out.'

Brooke was silent, puzzled.

'I never approved of those. I tried to

persuade Colin it was terribly wrong. But he . . . .'

'Colin!' Brooke stared. 'Colin did that? The wrecking of the motel gardens? The killing of Patricia Evans's plants?'

'I'm sorry. I'm truly sorry. For them as well as you. You — can tell them, if you want to. I don't think I have the courage for that.'

Brooke shook her head slowly. 'I won't tell them. They don't need to know, now. Not who it was. No one needs to know that. He must have hated me dreadfully.'

'He respected Damien, admired him — loved him as he would have loved a brother who was also his hero. I'm glad he never found out his idol had feet of very poor clay.'

'I think,' Brooke said, 'that's something most of Broadfell will find hard to come to terms with.'

Dianne Paton stood up to go, and Brooke held out her hand.

'Thank you for coming, Dianne. It took a lot of courage. Courage seems to be something the Patons have had in abundance. And remember: the past is just that. Past. The door isn't closed on our friendship.' She smiled. 'How can I feel resentment towards people who did nothing but use their common sense in reaching a logical conclusion about me?'

The other woman gripped her hand tightly for a moment. 'Thank you. I feel I need friends right now. But I don't need to tell you about that. You've needed friends also. Even more than I do. But you had too few when the need was greatest.'

She slipped out quietly and Brooke closed the door and stood very still for a minute. Freedom, she reflected — the freedom from suspicion, the freedom to go about her life without people glancing askance and silently wondering whether or not she was a murderer — that freedom would take everyone time to adjust to.

Perhaps herself most of all. She had expected it would be something she could embrace almost instantly, but she was finding the full realization of it was taking more time than she would have ever guessed. It was, as she had told Tom, like returning home after a very long absence and finding herself almost a stranger.

* * *

It was the following afternoon when Brooke remembered the two men.

She had no idea why the memory suddenly lurched into her consciousness, but evidently some part of the brain had quietly stored it.

She had lunched early at Maree's coffee shop. Normally she either had a quick lunch at home or, more commonly, took a sandwich and a thermos to work, whether in the office or out on a job. But on this day, doubtless as part of her light-hearted mood, she felt like indulging herself in the minor luxury of a salmon salad, with fruit juice and a chat with Maree, who was in sparkling mood with her own happiness with Harley. So, in a mood of cheerful contentment with the world, Brooke had driven down the range to a retirement village which had recently acquired more land and was in the process of building additional accommodation cottages, and had contracted Greenlands Landscaping to design the grounds and develop the lawns and trees and gardens.

She was looking at a newly paved courtyard and making notes on suitable plantings in beds and large tubs. Probably it was the automatic association of plants with Patricia's nursery, but abruptly in her mind she could see the two men who had been leaving just as she had arrived the previous morning — official-looking fellows with business shirts and ties and brief-cases — doing, Pat had said, some sort of survey. Unremarkable men, except that one of them had been wearing a tie with a distinctive cream and blue stripe and a tiger-eye agate tie pin, and she had seen him before.

She had seen him in her living-room, holding a knife and wearing a balaclava.

She stood rigid, shock holding her momentarily as helpless as if she had grasped a live electric wire. She was dimly aware that the retirement village manager, who had been walking around with her and discussing ideas, had said something, and she forced herself to turn her head and look at him.

'Sorry. I — I've just remembered something. Something terribly important. Or it may be. I have to make a phonecall. I'll get back to you, maybe tomorrow.'

He looked somewhat taken aback, but said only, 'Oh. All right.'

Brooke was already hurrying back towards her car, pulling out her mobile phone. She punched the number of Patricia's nursery.

'Pat,' she said urgently, 'it's Brooke. Listen. Those two men who were leaving the nursery just as I arrived yesterday morning. What exactly did they want?'

Sounding puzzled, Patricia said, 'They were just doing some sort of survey on nursery sales.'

'But did they seem interested in anything in particular?'

'Well, they weren't interested in the plants we deal in, only things like chemicals — weedicides, stuff like that. I don't carry much of that.'

'Poisons,' Brooke said doubtfully. 'Any particular poison?'

'No. Anyway, I don't keep anything highly toxic. Why?'

'Were they interested in anything else?'

'Actually, I suppose they asked more questions about fertilizers than anything else.'

Brooke frowned. A prickling of alarm, something beyond an understandable reaction to having seen one — and probably both — of the balaclava-clad invaders of her home, was stirring along her nerves; some vague, nameless, shapeless fear.

'Why, Brooke?' Patricia asked again. 'Is something wrong?'

'*Something* is,' Brooke said. 'I don't know what, but something might be very wrong indeed. I've only just remembered. One of those men was wearing a tie with a most unusual pattern, and a very distinctive tie-pin. And last time I saw him he was also wearing a balaclava.'

'Wearing a — Brooke! Are you sure?'

'As sure as I can be about anything. It can't be coincidence. They looked amused yesterday, when they met me in the doorway. But I thought they were simply amused at my high spirits. I was whistling, I remember. Pat, try to remember everything they said. Did they seem genuine?'

'Well, they had cards with 'Department of Primary Industries' printed on them, but I guess that doesn't prove anything. I was a bit surprised at their interest in fertilizer, but they had a logical explanation. I carry mainly organic fertilizer, but they seemed much keener to know how much nitrogenous stuff I sold, and who would buy it.'

'Go on,' Brooke urged. 'Try to remember exactly.'

'Why, Brooke?' Patricia asked again. 'What is it? What's wrong?'

'I don't know. Something's at the back of my mind, but I can't quite grasp it. Just tell me everything you can remember. It may be quite insignificant and I've just got a bad case of the jitters after realizing who they were.'

Patricia was silent a moment, thinking. 'They asked if they could look at my supply of organic fertilizer and I showed them. Then they asked if I had any ammonium nitrate and I said no. Then they wrote that down and asked how much I would have sold in the past four months, if I could recall approximately without checking records, and who would buy it — gardeners or farmers. I told them that was an easy question to answer: the Anglican minister had bought my entire stock — I think six bags. I'd never bothered to get any more in, as gardeners didn't ask for it much, and if anyone wanted it they could get it from the local farm-supplies store. They laughed and asked if I knew why in the world the Anglican minister would want six bags of fertilizer. I told them he was picking it up for a farmer who wanted it but was too ill to come in and get it.'

Brooke said, 'It sounds harmless enough. Did they ask anything else?'

'They asked the farmer's name because they were supposed to follow up fertilizer sales to find out what it was used for. I told them . . .'

Her voice trailed into silence.

'Pat?' Brooke said anxiously. 'Are you still there?'

'Yes.' Her voice was oddly flat.

'What is it? What's wrong?' It was Brooke's turn to ask now, feeling her uneasiness mounting to cold fear that was still formless.

'I told them,' Patricia said slowly, 'that I thought Damien had said it was for a Mr Martin, but I may have been mistaken, because the only farmer named Martin that I knew was in a nursing home and his farm was deserted, so Damien couldn't have been

214

buying it for him. But I'd told Damien if he wanted more than my five or six bags he could get it from Darrel Want at the farm-supplies store, so Darrel might know who Damien was buying for.'

She hesitated. 'Brooke, I hope to God I'm crazy. But when I think back, those men asked too many questions about nitrate of ammonia — wanted too many details.'

Brooke was still standing beside her car, the phone held to her ear, and the fear that had been rising inside her was no longer formless. It had taken shape with a terrible, sickening dread as the same thought crashed into her mind had obviously flooded Patricia's.

'You know what that stuff can be used for,' Patricia said grimly, 'quite apart from growing things?'

'Yes.' Brooke's voice was very quiet. 'I know.'

'And there was that padlocked shed out at Stewart Martin's farm, with the van parked inside and not looking neglected like you'd expect. Brooke, what if 'the stuff' those thugs demanded from you was *fertilizer*?'

'Like the Oklahoma bomb,' Brooke said very softly. 'Yes. Nitrogenous fertilizer mixed with a bit of diesel and given a detonating device can blow a hellish hole.'

'And yet,' Patricia said reasonably, 'why would they want the stuff Damien bought? It was no different from any other ammonium nitrate they could buy anywhere fertilizer is sold. It's hardly a restricted substance.'

'But,' Brooke said, thinking frantically, 'suppose Damien had already set it up, and the others didn't know how to do it if they had to begin again? And I'd guess they must need it soon.'

'But Brooke, why in the world would Damien want to make a *bomb*?'

'I don't know. I have not the faintest idea.'

'Look,' Patricia said reasonably, 'surely we're going off the deep end and being absurd. It's far more likely that Damien bought the fertilizer to oblige a sick farmer, just like he said, and although your balaclava-wearing friends are a couple of thugs who apparently thought Damien had a large parcel of drugs, they do in fact have government jobs and were in fact simply doing a legitimate survey. After all, presumably they must have jobs somewhere.'

'Logic tells me you're right, of course. We haven't a shred of anything to suggest otherwise. And yet Rachel — his mother — said Damien had to be killed to prevent him from committing what she called 'a monstrous evil', which everyone interpreted as meaning he planned to murder me. And yet that theory never really made much sense. It just seemed the only possible one. But what if Rachel meant something entirely different — a truly monstrously evil thing? Pat, I'm going out to Stewart Martin's farm to see if the van's still there. If it is, I might be able to get into the barn and perhaps see what's inside the van, or at least find out from the neighbouring farmer whether he knows anything about it. Then hopefully we can put to rest these horrors we've conjured up.'

She paused, and added, 'Or we'll have enough to warrant calling the police — something we certainly don't have at the moment. But I shan't rest till I know, one way or the other.'

'If you're going out there you might need help to get into the shed. I'll meet you there. In fact, Cameron's home today — the teachers are having one of their pupil-free days when they deal with work other than actual teaching. I remember there's a shutter window in the shed, and Cameron could probably nip through it easily if it's too small for us.'

'Thanks, Pat. But there's no need for you to drive out there. I have to come through Broadfell on my way, so I'll pick you and

Cameron up in about twenty minutes. I'm at The Willows retirement village.'

* * *

By the time she reached Patricia's nursery Brooke was feeling ridiculous, and said so.

'But we are going, aren't we?' Cameron said anxiously, having been told a little of the reason for the expedition. 'I bet I can get through that window easily, and I bet that van is full of stuff from burglaries, or a bank hold-up, even. I've told Chips he can't come today because he can't climb through windows. We are going, aren't we?'

Brooke smiled. 'Yes, we'll go, but I suspect it's the silliest wild-goose chase I've ever been on.'

Patricia said quietly, 'Let's just hope so.'

Brooke glanced at her friend's serious face. 'Has something else happened?'

'While I was waiting for you to come, I phoned Darrel Want at his farm-supplies place and asked him if the fellows had been to see him, asking about fertilizer. He said yes, and that those government fat cats are nothing but a pain, and I gather he as good as told them so. I guess it really wasn't my business, but I asked him if Damien had bought any fertilizer.'

218

She paused, and Brooke said, 'And?'

'Darrel said yes, just a week or so before he was killed. Darrel asked why I wanted to know, and I said I just wondered, because Damien had said he wanted it for a farmer who was sick, and I hadn't had much of the fertilizer he wanted. Darrel said yes, that was right, that's what Damien told him he wanted it for, because old Stewart Martin had arranged for someone to spread it, and as far as Darrel remembered he'd taken ten or twelve bags and paid cash. And took it away in an old white van.'

Brooke drove in silence for a while, and then said, 'And of course by far the most probable answer is that it was indeed for old Mr Martin, who could have been as insistent about that as he was about his rose — because he thinks the farm is still functioning and he'll soon be home again, and the neighbour who's looking after the place would spread the fertilizer for him. Which has probably been done, and the neighbour simply returned Stewart Martin's van to the shed and locked it up for safety.'

'You mean I don't even get to go in through the window and look for loot, or anything?' Cameron's disgust was obvious.

'We'll go and see the neighbour first, and ask if he knows all about the van,' Brooke

219

said. Relenting at Cameron's crestfallen silence, she added, 'But maybe we could go out to the farm afterwards and just make sure it's all right.'

To Cameron's unabashed delight, Stewart Martin's neighbours proved not to be at home, so Brooke drove on out to the deserted farm. Cameron hopped out to open the gate into the area where the old farm-buildings stood.

There were no cattle in sight, so Brooke said, 'You can leave the gate open, Cameron. We won't be long.'

They drove in and parked the car beside the barn. Everything was as derelict and overgrown as before. Patricia glanced across to the tumbledown fence which had once enclosed the house and garden, and she smiled.

'There are a couple of flowers on Mr Martin's rose. Maybe we could take them back for him, if we've anything to cut them with.'

'I've got my pocket-knife,' Cameron volunteered.

'Good,' Brooke said. 'Then we can probably get the roses.' She looked at the barn, still padlocked. 'Nothing seems to have changed.'

'There's been a vehicle in and out fairly

recently,' Patricia pointed out. 'You can see the wheel-tracks in the grass.'

'Someone's using the barn, then,' Brooke said, sounding relieved. 'Probably the van belongs to the neighbour who leases the property, and he's taken it away, or else he just leaves it here for some reason.'

They peered through the chinks between the weather-boards, and could see the van was still there. The wooden shutter window Patricia had remembered was quite small, but Cameron reached up and got his fingers under the edge of it against the sill, and tugged.

'It'll be latched on the inside, I guess,' Brooke said.

Cameron shook his head. 'I don't think it is, I can slide my fingers right along. I think it's just stuck. If we could pull it open I could easily get in, and I could look through the back windows of the van and see for sure what's inside. Aw, come on,' he urged, as the two women hesitated.

'We really haven't any right whatever to do this,' Brooke said. 'But — well, it can't do any harm, to settle it in our minds. Looking won't hurt anything.'

She and Patricia worked their fingers under the frame of the shutter and pulled, and with a protesting squeak of wood on wood it reluctantly opened outwards.

'I can get through there easily,' Cameron declared cheerfully, eyeing the small rectangle of space.

'I'll give you a leg up,' his mother offered, but he was already scrambling through, scrabbling at the weather-board wall with his sneakers.

He dropped down lightly inside and said, 'I hope there are glass windows at the back, so's I can see inside.'

In a moment he announced, 'No, they're metal, like the sides. I can't see in, and they're locked.' He walked around the van and said, 'The next-door farmer must have driven it recently. It's not dusty or anything. It's a bit rusty, though — well, just in one spot, actually. Can you see, Mum? In the bottom of this panel there's a funny-shaped patch of rust, like a perfect map of South America. See?'

'It is, too,' Patricia agreed, smiling. 'All right, Cameron, better come out again.'

'Hang on,' he said, peering at the patch of rust. 'South America's actually rusted through, just around about Brazil. There's a little hole.' He bent close. 'There's a bag of something right up against it.'

'What sort of bag?' Patricia asked.

'One of those woven plastic bags.'

Brooke's stomach muscles were tense.

'Cameron,' Patricia said calmly, 'you said you had your pocket-knife with you. Open a blade and see if you can make a tiny hole in the bag by pushing the knife-blade through the rust-hole.'

'No prob,' he said happily. 'But I mightn't be able to tell what's inside the bag. I mean, if it's stolen televisions or something.'

He carefully inserted a blade through the rust-hole, which was about the diameter of an index-finger, and twisted the knife in a drilling action. As he drew the blade away a tiny trickle of small pellets followed it.

He picked some up from the dusty concrete floor and sniffed them and rolled them in his fingers.

'It's only fertilizer!' he said in total disgust.

The two women looked at each other. 'Which might mean anything or nothing,' Brooke said softly. 'All right, Cameron, you'd better come out again.'

'Just before you do,' Patricia said, 'is the floor pretty dusty? It looks to be.'

'Yes, it is.'

'Can you see tyre-marks, as if the van's been out lately? You said the van itself isn't dusty.'

'No, it's real clean. But no, there don't seem to be any tyre-marks. Lots of footprints, though.'

'Are you sure?' Brooke asked. 'I mean, do they look fresh?'

'Oh, yes. Mostly around the engine, but all over the place. You can see there were two different kinds of boots, too,' he said proudly, pleased with his powers of detection. 'Looks like someone's changed the battery. There's one here against the wall, and it hasn't got dust or cobwebs or anything on it.'

'Good man,' Patricia said. 'Better come out now, though.'

'All that, and all that's in there is fertilizer.' Cameron's disappointment was obvious. 'There's a pile of old sacks in the corner,' he added hopefully. 'Maybe there's something hidden under those. I'll just have a look.'

'You be careful,' his mother said sharply. 'There might be a snake, or red-back spiders. I think you'd better leave the sacks alone and come out.'

'Wait, Cameron,' Brooke said quickly. She touched Patricia's arm and nodded toward the farm-track. A white Ford Falcon sedan drove towards them and stopped in the gateway, neatly blocking it.

Fear shot along her nerves.

'Cameron,' she said softly, 'we're in trouble. Get under that pile of sacks, cover yourself with them and don't move, no matter what happens. Understand? *No matter what happens*. There are two men getting out of a car. Bad men. Very bad. One has a gun. Stay hidden until you're sure they're gone. This is not a game.'

She risked a glance through the window and saw Cameron scuttle away to the corner. Please God, keep him safe she thought desperately. It's too late to help Pat. I got them into this. Heaven forgive me for letting them get involved. In whatever it is.

The two men walked without haste across the fifty metres from the gateway again dressed neatly, one in grey slacks, one in navy, white shirts, ties. A different tie today, but the same tie-pin. Ordinary men going about some ordinary business, one may have thought, except that one carried a shot-gun.

No brief-cases today, Brooke thought bitterly, but the same camouflaging dark glasses. One with a shot-gun and the other with a large duffel-bag. She wondered what was in the bag.

'Well, well.' The man with the agate tie-pin looked amused. For some reason Brooke found that much more frightening than if he had been angry.

'The clever Mrs Hardwick and her clever friend finally figured out what we were looking for. What a shame you left it too late.'

'What on earth are you talking about?'

Brooke demanded in a desperate attempt at bluff. 'And why, may I ask, are you walking around with a shot-gun? Who are you, anyway?' She tried to keep the terror out of her voice. Whether it showed in her face she didn't know.

'It's all right, Brooke,' Patricia said, carrying on the attempt at bluff with all the polish of a seasoned actress. 'These are the DPI men who are checking on the use of fertilizers. I expect you find you sometimes need a gun if you stumble on a poisonous snake when you're out in the paddocks, don't you, gentlemen?'

'Poisonous snakes or anything else that threatens us,' the shorter man said, still smiling. 'But why ever are you ladies out in a place like this on a working day?'

'The old gentleman who owns this farm asked me to get one of his special roses for him,' Brooke said. 'And sometimes it's a good idea to take a little time off work.'

'Oh, of course. And why were you looking around the barn?'

'Is there a reason we shouldn't?'

'Tomorrow,' he said 'there wouldn't have been any reason at all. But today it's most unfortunate for you.'

He shook his head mockingly. 'Because you've seen us here, and we certainly can't afford to be identified. Your attempts at bluff do you credit, but will do you no good.'

He looked squarely at Brooke. 'You recognized us yesterday, at the nursery, didn't you? And you two put your heads together and started thinking. I must congratulate you on reaching a conclusion so quickly.'

Brooke said bitterly, 'I didn't recognize you, not yesterday. Afterwards, I remembered your tie and tie-pin.'

He stared, then laughed. 'Good God. Something so damned simple, and it will cost you your lives.'

'But I should have recognized you earlier,' Brooke said. 'Shouldn't I? Because quite apart from that day in my house, we've met. But of course I couldn't recognize you then, because I hadn't seen your face. You were afraid I might recognize your voice, weren't you? You're from the New Day community. You were gardening, and you were wearing a hat. I've only just remembered. People look different in a hat. Brother George introduced us. You're Donald. So suppose you tell us just what that New Day group is really about. If you're going to kill us, we've a right to know why.'

Play for time, she thought; it's not likely to help, but there's always a chance; play for time, and pray.

'The New Day group?' Donald laughed harshly, and in an instant his whole demeanour changed. 'What a spineless, useless lot. Oh, I went there with high hope. An anti-drug community, I thought: wonderful. Someone to really take up the fight and make a difference. I thought I'd find some among them who'd help me form a real group, with real punch.'

There was sudden anger, seething, insane anger in his voice and glittering in his blue eyes.

'And how many did I find?' he went on. 'How many who had enough guts to be ready to really do something? I'll tell you how many: Jack, here.' He jerked his head at the man with the shot-gun. 'Jack came to the group. I had one ally. Then your husband came. Damien Hardwick. He had come looking for committed people, too. He came searching because he had been told by God to destroy those who promote the use of drugs in any way. Any way. He told us the opportunity was coming when we could strike such a blow against this wickedness that our deed would reverberate around the world and make it clear to everyone that dealing or wanting to make drugs easy-to-get carried a price.'

His voice had taken on a weird, almost evangelical ring.

'It would carry a terrible price — a price so high that eventually no one would be prepared to risk paying it.'

Brooke was staring at him. It was as if he was another man altogether — not even like the man he'd been the day the two of them had been waiting to ambush her in her own home. If he'd been like this that day, she thought, he'd have killed me then.

'We will make such an impact,' he went on gloatingly, 'that others will join up — like-minded people all over the country — all over the world. We don't need many people. Just a handful who are truly committed.'

Keep him talking, was all Brooke could think of; maybe I'll get an idea; maybe someone will chance to come.

Her own fear for herself was shrunk to insignificance by her anguish for Patricia and her terror that Cameron would be discovered. She was standing beside Patricia, and she reached out and gripped her friend's hand. She couldn't even guess the agony of fear for Cameron that his mother must be feeling.

'I'm sorry, Pat,' she said unsteadily.

'It's not your fault,' Patricia said quietly. 'I told them. I virtually told them where the stuff was.'

'You couldn't have known who they were,

or why they wanted to know,' Brooke answered.

Donald was still talking about his grand plan as if he were totally unaware they were speaking to each other.

Brooke looked around. The derelict sheds, the nearby trees and a close, thick patch of bush might have offered enough cover to risk a dash for life that one of them might have made successfully if they ran. It was only a single-shot shot-gun. But Cameron was in the barn, and leaving him was unthinkable.

The man called Jack shifted the shot-gun. 'Time we were making a move,' he said. 'May as well kill them now so we can get on with things.'

'No,' Donald said quickly. 'There's a chance the bodies might be found quite soon. We don't want any sort of hue and cry raised, even though there's no way of linking us to it. Someone might hear the shots and come to investigate, because there shouldn't be anyone here. We'll take them with us.'

'Take them with us?' Jack echoed in alarm.

'Gagged and trussed up, in the back of the van. That way, they'll simply disappear. Literally.'

Jack stared, and then laughed. 'You're not wrong. Yes, top idea. We've got plenty of tape. What about their car?'

Donald shrugged. 'Just leave it. It'll remain one of Australia's most puzzling disappearances.'

He turned to look at the two women again.

'You see,' he said, 'as you've no doubt worked out for yourselves by now, the van is going to be a mobile bomb. There's more than half a tonne of fertilizer in there, enough for a huge explosion once we add the final touches. We didn't know anything about making a bomb, but Damien learned how.'

I can just imagine him at the local stone quarry when there was blasting in progress, Brooke thought grimly; delightful, fascinated, easily charming the explosives expert — who happened to be a member of Damien's congregation — into explaining how the charges were set up, and how other means of blasting could be concocted. After all, who would hesitate to chat about it with someone as harmless as the Anglican minister? The man in charge of blasting operations knew Damien; would never suspect him of anything but innocent interest.

'He set it all up for us, just before he was killed,' Donald was explaining. 'Attached the detonating device — he talked about something called power gel, I remember, and said one stick of gelignite would be plenty — and he attached the timer and told us what we have to do. But he never told us where he'd hidden the van. He said the fewer people who knew about it, the better. When he was killed we thought you'd done it because you'd found out his plans.'

Bound and gagged, tied in a van with half a tonne of explosives, waiting to be blown to fragments. Brooke shut her eyes for a second, and gripped Patricia's hand more tightly. She swallowed against the dryness in her throat.

'What — what is it you and he planned?' The voice that spoke the words in a harsh near-whisper didn't sound like hers at all.

'We are going to start a new war against drugs, with a new weapon: terrorism. At seven-thirty tonight this van will explode against a wall in Brisbane and will echo around the world. Many will die. All we have to do is to pour a little diesel into each bag of the stuff, set the timer, park the van beside the building and leave. Oh,' he said with a mirthless laugh, 'the party will end with a bang.'

'If what you're saying is true,' Patricia said, the steadiness of her voice obviously belying what she must be feeling, 'why was the bomb set up all those months ago? And why wasn't Damien going to drive the van himself? He dumped you right in it, didn't he? He wasn't going to take any risks, was he?' She was deliberately baiting the man, trying to turn his anger against Damien.

'The launch of our campaign was to have happened months ago, but it was postponed,' Donald said coldly. 'And Damien couldn't drive the van himself. He was too easily recognized in this area.'

'You won't be allowed near any special function in this van,' Brooke told him. 'If that's what you're planning.'

'Oh, I think we will,' Donald said, abruptly cheerful. 'Wait till you see what it looks like when we dress it up.'

An even sharper jolt of fear hit with sickening force. They were going to do something to change the appearance of the van. That meant, almost certainly, that they'd be working inside the barn. How much chance was there that Cameron wouldn't be discovered? How long could a not quite-ten-year-old lie still and silent under a pile of dusty, mouldy sacks?

Donald had set the duffel-bag down and taken a key from his pocket and was unlocking the padlocked chain that fastened the doors. He dropped the chain to one side and pulled the big double doors open. Then he unzipped the bag and took out a large roll of heavy-duty, fabric-impregnated adhesive tape.

'It'll take two of us to get these signs on straight,' he told Jack, 'so I'll just fasten these nice ladies so they don't get any funny ideas about running away or being heroic.'

'It'd still be simpler to kill them before we put them in the van.'

'Simpler, but a degree of risk. This way there's no risk at all.'

Donald, Brooke was beginning to think, was just finding excuses. He wasn't keen on violence he would have to witness. A bomb with a timing device that allowed him to be well away from the horrors when they happened was much more in his line. Jack, on the other hand, would have no such squeamishness. But Donald was the dominant personality, and he was in charge.

He came over to her. 'Put your wrists together.' He swiftly wrapped the adhesive tape several times around her wrists, binding them tightly together. Then he knelt and did the same with her ankles, and repeated the process on Patricia. Jack, gun half-raised, watched. No one spoke.

Brooke couldn't know exactly what Patricia must be feeling, beyond unspeakable fear for her son. But for her own part Brooke experienced a wave of near-panic at being left standing but rendered helplessly immobile, even though for all practical purposes they were no more helpless than before. Somehow, it was different, and she felt sweat break out all over her body.

For God's sake, she thought, kill us now and get it over with. But she kept silent.

Jack put the gun down beside the door. Donald had taken a roll of plastic about forty-five centimetres wide from the duffel-bag, and they unrolled it between them, revealing it to be a self-adhesive sign about one and a half metres long, with red lettering. The van, Brooke realized, was about to acquire a prominent logo to give its presence, wherever it was going, apparent legitimacy.

From where she and Patricia were standing she couldn't read the lettering. The two men went to the driver's side of the van and carefully aligned the sign and fixed it smoothly into place and sealed the edges with the adhesive tape. Only a close examination would reveal that it wasn't a proper, ducoed part of the paintwork.

Please God, let them leave it at that, Brooke thought desperately; don't let them put a sign on the other side.

Cameron's concealing sacks were in a corner on the other side of the van. If they walked around there they would almost tread on him. He had held his nerve superbly. He still had a chance.

Jack reached into the duffel-bag and brought out a matching sign. They carefully attached it to the passenger side of the van. Nothing happened.

Then Donald stepped back to admire their work, and stepped on the pile of sacks, and sprang back.

'What the bloody hell . . . ' he began, and Cameron leapt to his feet, covered in dust, scattering hessian sacks, and ran.

10

The surprise was almost complete.

But Cameron had been lying rigidly still for what must have seemed half an eternity, and he emerged from the heavy darkness of his hiding-place to the brightness of a sunlit late-afternoon. Half-blinded by the sudden emergence into light, and with cramp taking the edge off his normal eel-like suppleness, he stumbled over the duffel-bag and before he could regain full balance Jack grabbed him.

He struggled gamely and kicked out, but Jack hit him a stunning blow to the side of his head that made his mother cry out, 'No! Please! Don't.'

Donald caught hold of him also, and between them they held him helpless. He looked at his mother and Brooke with despair in his face.

'Sorry, Mum,' he said.

'Oh, Cameron, darling, it's not your fault,' Patricia said, trying to fight tears. 'You were wonderful. You almost did it.'

'You did a grand job,' Brooke agreed, trying to keep her own voice steady. 'You're a solid-gold hero.'

And, looking at him, she knew he had heard enough of what had been said for his highly intelligent mind to know they were about to go on a journey from which there wasn't going to be a return. With a dreadful ache in her heart she thought: for Pat and me it's rough enough — but Cameron! At nine years old, and all life untouched before him.

The men marched him over to stand beside the women, and fastened his wrists and ankles in the same way. It was incredible, Brooke thought, how strong several layers of that tape was. She had been steadily trying to stretch it by forcing outwards with both wrists and ankles, but it was without the least result.

Cameron looked up at Patricia, white faced. 'Do you think someone will look after Chips?'

Oh, God, Brooke thought, even now his first thought is for his dog.

'Yes, of course,' Patricia said. 'Barnaby and Jessica love him. They'll make sure he's just fine. And there's Maree, and Harley, and Mr Alford — they'd all look after him.'

Donald had now taken a white dust-coat out of the duffel-bag and put it on. Embroidered on the pocket in red were the words 'North Star Fire and Security Service'. He got into the van and backed it out of the shed to reveal the same lettering boldly obvious on the sides. Jack shut the doors but didn't padlock them, and threw the chain and padlock into the duffel-bag.

Donald hopped down from the cabin and unlocked the rear doors of the van. Inside were the bags of fertilizer, neatly stacked, about fourteen of them, Brooke calculated.

They didn't fill the van completely, and Donald said quite cheerfully, 'Right. Now we'll just gag you three, and then load you in. We don't want you making lots of noise when we stop, do we?'

Brooke tried one last bluff. 'Other people knew we were coming here this afternoon, and then going on to visit the New Day community. When we disappear it will lead the police straight to the community, with lots of questions. It could prove most unfortunate for you, because it won't take anyone long to get very suspicious about you in connection with this, and with the outrage you're planning. You'll destroy yourselves. Stop now, while you've a chance. You haven't done anything terribly serious yet. Disarm your bomb and let us go. You can disable my car, and by the time we walk to the nearest house, you can be well away. It's your only chance, because the police will go at once to the New Day community. You'll never

239

succeed in this crazy plan of starting a terrorist group.'

'You're lying,' Donald said. 'You weren't going to the community.'

Cameron instantly said, 'Brooke doesn't tell lies. We *were* going there. Mum told me.'

'That's right,' Patricia agreed.

Bless you both, Brooke thought.

The two men were staring from one of their captives to another, faintly unsure.

Brooke went on, 'You can't afford not to go back to the community, at least for a while, if you go ahead with this madness. You can't afford to draw attention to yourselves by disappearing straight away. And once it's known that we didn't arrive there, and our car is found here, your car-tread tracks on the dirt road will be picked up. And that car belongs at the community, and everyone there knows it's yours. It'll be checked. How will you explain why you were here?'

The argument, she knew, was as full of holes as the proverbial sieve, but a faintly flickering hope of their reaction was stirring her to pile bluff on bluff, and improbability on improbability. Please, she thought. Please take the bait.

There were a few seconds of silence.

'All right,' Donald said curtly. 'You've got a mobile phone, I suppose?'

'In the glove box of the car.'

'I'll get it. Call someone and tell them there's been a change of plan. You're not going to the community after all. Something's come up — anything you like. But tell them you're going away for a few days. All three of you. You had an opportunity to take a week's holiday, or you had a call from a sick relative — anything. Just make it convincing.'

He brought the phone from the car. 'Tell me the number and I'll punch it in.' He glared at her. 'No tricks,' he snapped, 'or the kid will pay dearly. And remember, I'll be right here to hear every word on both sides of the conversation.'

'No tricks,' she told him, and recited Maree's coffee shop number, conscious of the puzzled stares of Patricia and Cameron.

Months before, while Damien was alive and Brooke had had a brooding fear of him, she had appealed earnestly to Maree, without telling her the reasons behind her fear. She had said then, 'Maree, I might at some time be in serious trouble — real trouble of the dangerous kind. If ever I phone you and say the words, 'I won't be able to come in for coffee after all', it will mean I need help. Police help. Please listen then very carefully to what I'll say, because I'll try to give you some clues as to what's

241

happening, without seeming to.'

Maree had been horrified. 'Brooke! What's wrong?'

'I can't tell you, not at present. And if I ever do use that code: 'I won't be able to come in for coffee after all', you must — you *must*, please — just answer as though there's nothing strange going on, you're just responding to what I'm saying. The full conversation might be overheard.'

'Oh, God,' Maree had said. 'I hope it never happens.'

'So do I,' Brooke had answered grimly.

But that had been a good many months ago, and the situation now was far different. What hope was there that Maree would remember enough to react quickly? Would she remember at all? It was asking too much.

'It's ringing,' Donald said tersely, and held the phone to Brooke's ear, with his own ear hatefully close by.

'Maree's coffee shop, Maree speaking,' said a cheerful voice.

With a silent prayer, Brooke answered. 'Maree, it's Brooke. Listen, I won't be able to come in for coffee after all.'

There was a silence of about three seconds. It felt like three hours.

'Oh, what a shame,' Maree said. 'Have you been held up somewhere?'

A very neat double-edged question that sounded totally innocent, Brooke thought. For what it was worth in terms of getting help, Maree had understood. God bless her quick wits.

'Yes, sort of. Patricia and Cameron and I were all going to visit the New Day community this afternoon, as you know, but our plans are changed and we're going away for a break. It came up quite unexpectedly through business — one of those promotional prize gimmicks.'

I've got to make it sound feasible, she thought — not for Maree, but for these creatures. 'It's one of those things companies promoting their products throw at you sometimes, usually hoping you don't take them, I guess. But we'd be crazy not to go along with this offer. It's a fully financed break for a few days. Can you look after things?'

'I'll do my best, Brooke.' Maree's voice was carefully controlled. 'Can you tell me where you're going?'

'Oh, the country first — a nice quiet place where we went once before. Then Brisbane for a short time, where the plan is we'll visit Aunt Eileen.'

There was a moment's silence. 'I see. Are you doing a farm stay sort of thing? That place where we all went once, where they had the lovely roses?'

You beautiful person, Brooke thought.

'Yes,' she said brightly. 'Thanks for being so understanding, Maree. You're a champion. Tell Tom — '

Donald clicked the phone off and put it in his pocket, and checked his watch.

'Right. We've wasted too much time already. Just as well we gave ourselves an early start to allow for delays. Jack, is there another roll of that tape in the bag?'

'Sure.' He rummaged, and Donald turned to his prisoners.

'I'll just check your pockets for handkerchiefs or tissues.'

None of them spoke as he felt swiftly in their pockets, removed Cameron's pocket-knife with a grunt of satisfaction, retrieved a handkerchief from each, folded Brooke's roughly and fastened it over her mouth with the heavy tape wrapped right around her head.

Then he did the same to Patricia and Cameron. The frightening sense of helplessness Brooke had felt at having her hands and feet bound was a trifle compared with the awful sense of finality, of total hopelessness, which was created by being gagged.

She and Patricia looked at each other, and she could sense in her friend the same feeling of despair. She knew that Patricia would guess she had tried to alert Maree to the fact they were in trouble, but Pat could have no idea whether or not Maree had seemed to understand.

And, Brooke thought bitterly, what difference could it make, however much Maree had guessed? She had realized they were at, or being taken to, Stewart Martin's farm. But they would be gone long before anyone could get here, and after that they would be untraceable, and Maree could have no idea of the existence of the van-bomb.

Cameron, his eyes dark with fear, fought the gag, twisting his head from side to side, until Jack grabbed him by the collar and clouted him hard over the side of his face, bringing a heavily muffled cry of wordless protest from his mother. Half-stunned, Cameron stood still, with Jack holding him, one hand on his collar, the other gripping a fistful of his hair.

Then the two men picked Brooke up — Donald taking her by the arms and Jack grasping her by the feet — and unceremoniously dumped her into the back of the van, and followed the same procedure with Patricia and Cameron.

'We'll have to fix their feet,' Jack commented. 'They could make a bit of a racket by kicking against the side of the van. Might be heard once the van is stopped.'

'You're right,' Donald agreed. 'Sit side by side and close together, backs against those bags,' he ordered. 'Pull your feet back, knees bent.'

They struggled into position. 'Now, if anyone has any ideas about trying to kick me, Jack will put a shot-gun blast through your knee.'

No one doubted that he meant it. He passed the tape between Brooke's arms and around the wrist-bindings, then pulled it down taut and tied it tightly around the ankle-bindings, so that she was fixed in an almost foetal position. Then he did the same with the others.

Satisfied they were completely helpless, he shifted some of the bags, took out the pocket-knife he had been using to cut the tape, carefully cut through a section of one bag of the fertilizer that was on the floor and scooped out some of the pellets. Jack handed him two five-litre cans. He unscrewed the cap of the first and a heavy smell of diesel escaped as Donald gently poured a little of the fuel over the contents of the bag.

There was a small box on the floor of the van and he removed the lid and carefully and methodically set the time on an ordinary-looking alarm clock to seven-thirty, replaced the lid and tucked it into the bag. Then he restacked the other bags of fertilizer beside and on top, first slitting each and pouring diesel in until every bag had diesel added to the fertilizer. He took a deep breath and stepped back, breathing heavily.

'It's done,' he said. 'Nothing can stop it now.' There was throbbing excitement in his voice and in his eyes. 'Just over two hours from now, at seven-thirty this evening, the world will find there's a new weapon in the war against drugs. Something more effective than all the police forces: terrorism. This is the beginning.'

Brooke wanted to scream at him: You fool! How many innocent people, sincere and well-meaning people, is this thing going to kill? What does terrorism achieve, except terror? It will do far more harm than the drugs you're trying to fight. You try to fight evil with evil, hoping good will come of it, but far too regularly no good comes, and all that is left is the evil.

But even if she had been able to speak, she knew he would never listen.

The rear doors were slammed shut and locked, and they were in almost total darkness. Two small gratings for air-vents, high in the metal sides of the van, showed a faint glimmer of late sunlight.

They heard Donald say, 'Keep the van in sight from the car, but don't make it obvious that we're travelling together. When I pull into the hotel, just drive past and park where we arranged. I'll shed the coat and walk across. We should be a good half-hour away before it happens.'

'It's still a mistake to take them there alive,' Jack insisted. 'Take one of the small roads into the forestry plantations. I'll follow you in and finish them there. You can go for a walk while I do it, if you want. If they haven't already suffocated by then. In either case, no one can link us to it there. The bodies can stay in the van and still vanish.'

His tone was quietly persuasive.

'It's a risk,' Donald said.

'Less risk than taking them all the way alive, just in case they can somehow attract attention.'

'There's the time factor,' Donald objected. 'We've lost enough time already.'

'There's no point in arriving too early.'

Donald hesitated. 'All right. It'll have to depend on how well we're doing for time. If there's time, I'll pull into that road where we saw that accident a few weeks ago. Get up close enough to see me when we get near there.'

'Right.' Jack laughed. 'Drive carefully. You don't want an overzealous cop checking your van.'

They heard his footsteps going away, and Donald slid into the cabin of the van, shut the door and started the motor.

The final two hours had begun.

★   ★   ★

Maree put the handset back in its cradle on the wall-mounted phone, and stood for several seconds gripping the edge of the counter, shocked into numbness and telling herself she had to think.

'Think, you fool, think fast!' she muttered.

The older of the two ladies who helped in the coffee shop, Elaine, who did most of the cooking, turned sharply.

'Maree! What in the world is wrong? You're white as a sheet! It's not Harley?'

Harley was a great favourite with Maree's staff, his easygoing friendliness an instant hit with them.

Maree shook her head. 'No. It's Brooke. Brooke Hardwick. Something's terribly wrong and I have to get it straight in my head. Elaine, can you and Frances lock up? It's closing-time. I have to make phonecalls.'

She punched the triple zero emergency number as she spoke, and asked the swiftly answering voice for the police.

A voice told her he was Constable Wilkinson, and she hurriedly told him her name and address.

'I'm reporting an abduction. Two women and a nine-year-old boy have been abducted from a derelict farm off Petersham Road near Broadfell.'

'You saw this happen? How long ago?'

'A few minutes.'

'What sort of vehicle were they taken in? What, exactly happened?'

'I don't know. She couldn't tell me any details, because obviously they were listening.'

'She? Madam, take a deep breath and try to tell me just what you know.'

Maree tried to speak steadily. 'Believe me,' she begged. 'Please listen and believe me. I didn't see it happen. One of the women — Brooke Hardwick — managed to phone me, using her mobile phone. She had to tell me in a sort of code.'

There was a moment's silence as Constable Wilkinson evidently considered this and undoubtedly wondered whether he was listening to a genuine emergency, a hoax, or hysteria.

'Suppose,' he said calmly, 'you begin at the beginning.'

'Look,' Maree said desperately, 'I can't tell you any more. I don't know why they were taken or who may have done it. All I can tell you is that two masked men broke into Mrs Hardwick's house some months ago and demanded something they believed she had. She didn't know what they wanted. She assumed it was drugs. Weeks ago we — myself and the three I mentioned, Mrs Hardwick, Mrs Evans and Cameron Evans — had occasion to visit Stewart Martin's deserted farm. He's an invalid. Apparently Brooke and Patricia Evans and Cameron went out there today. I don't know why. But, from what she was able to say without any listener understanding, they've been abducted there and are being taken to Brisbane.'

Maree gulped and added, 'Where she expects they will be killed.'

'She told you all this in such a way that no one who was listening would understand?' the constable asked doubtfully.

'Oh, for God's sake!' Maree exploded. 'There's not time to go into details. Get someone out there to stop those thugs!'

'We'll have someone out there as soon as possible. We'll need to speak — '

'I'll be out at the farm. Remember: Stewart Martin's farm off Petersham Road, near Broadfell.'

She cut the connection and dialled Harley's pharmacy, only to be told Mr Wilson had had to go to Nambour to keep a dental appointment at four forty-five. He wouldn't be coming back to the shop today as they were just closing up now; he'd go straight home.

Maree looked at her watch. With a dental appointment as late as that, Harley wouldn't be home for perhaps as much as another half-hour. She flipped pages in the telephone directory to find Tom Alford's number, her hands shaking so much she could barely trace her finger steadily enough down the column of names. She took a long, deep breath. You've got to hang together, she told herself; you *must*.

Tom answered cheerfully, and Maree thought with a flash of anguish that it might be a long time before he would sound happy again, unless she was very mistaken about his feelings for Brooke.

'Tom, it's Maree. Listen, there's no time to go into details, but I need you to come with me out to Stewart Martin's farm on Petersham Road. Brooke is in trouble — terrible trouble. I've called the police. I'll tell you on the way.'

'Wait at the coffee shop. I'll pick you up.' He slammed the phone down, and in something under two minutes he pulled up in the street beside her.

'I know where Petersham Road is, but not the farm. Give me directions when we're close,' he said crisply as the car swung out from the kerb. 'Now tell me what's wrong.'

He said nothing as Maree told him of Brooke's phonecall, but his jaw was rigid and he drove with the fierce concentration of a racing-driver.

Presently he said, 'Did you get the impression Brooke was forced to make that call?'

'No. I rather think she must have conned them into letting her do it.'

'You think there was more than one abductor?'

'There'd almost have to be, surely, to take three people.'

'Unless he had a gun at Cameron's head, or a knife at his throat,' Tom said grimly. 'Brooke and Patricia would do anything he said in that case.'

'Yes,' Maree said slowly. 'It's just that I keep remembering the two thugs Brooke called the balaclavas, who broke into her house and smashed up my shop to try to make her tell them where something was. I can't help thinking it's them. We're near the turn-off to the farm,' she added. 'There

— those two white posts up ahead.'

Tom swung the car on to the narrow farm-road. Tree shadows were just beginning to lengthen in the hot, midsummer late-afternoon, but there would be another hour and a half of daylight. The gate was open.

'That's Brooke's car beside the barn,' Maree said, feeling sick, the dread of what they might find mingling with the positive knowledge that she had understood at least some of what Brooke had been trying to tell her.

Tom stopped beside Brooke's car and leapt out, quickly looking in through the windows. But the car was empty, the doors closed but the locks not pushed down, the key still in the ignition.

'Don't touch the car,' Tom warned. 'Just in case there are prints that are of some use. I'll have a look around.'

'There's a car coming,' Maree said urgently, fear clutching at her.

It was a police car, lights flashing, coming fast. For all his apparently doubting attitude, Constable Wilkinson had acted swiftly and seriously. Two uniformed men got out of the car and hurried forward.

'Senior Constable Redford, this is Constable Bellingham, Nambour police. We were nearby, on another matter,' the older of the

254

two men said quickly. 'And you are?'

'I'm Maree Stewart, who raised the alarm. This is Tom Alford, a friend who brought me here. This is Mrs Hardwick's car. We haven't touched it.'

He nodded. 'How long have you been here?'

'A couple of minutes. We didn't meet any vehicle leaving the farm.'

'Tell me what you know.'

Maree went quickly through the facts of the phonecall again.

'Why are you certain that call should be taken at anything but its face value?'

'For one thing,' Tom cut in tersely, 'someone does not simply take off on a holiday, without warning, leaving their car unlocked, keys in the ignition, at a deserted farm.'

'Nothing about the phonecall made sense if taken at its face value,' Maree said. 'Listen. Months ago, while Brooke's husband was still alive, she told me that if she ever phoned me and used the words 'I won't be able to come in for coffee after all', it would be a signal that she was in danger, and I was to pay careful attention to anything else she said, because our conversation might be overheard. She would try to tell me what sort of trouble she was in, without letting anyone who was listening know what she meant — she'd be saying things with a kind of double meaning which I would understand. I didn't know then what on earth she was afraid of, but I later learned she was afraid of her husband.'

Maree was fighting to speak steadily, desperate to convince the officers she wasn't hysterical. 'After her husband was killed I didn't think any more about what she'd asked me to do. Not until this afternoon.'

'You said,' the senior constable said, 'that Mrs Hardwick believed they would be killed after they went to Brisbane. What grounds do you have for believing she meant that?'

'She said, 'the plan is we'll visit Aunt Eileen'. Brooke's Aunt Eileen was my fiancé's mother. She's been dead for some years. Please, you have to do something. Can't you set up road-blocks?'

'First, we'd need to know what sort of vehicle they're travelling in. And there are two main routes they could take. Can you imagine the difficulties of stopping and searching hundreds upon hundreds of vehicles on one major highway, let alone the less-used, old highway? No one can order that without good reason.'

'The good reason,' Tom Alford said with an obvious effort to keep his voice calm, 'is that three lives are in danger.'

'May be in danger,' the senior constable countered. 'Your friends must have had a reason to come out here today. Have you any idea what it might have been? Would they have come on a picnic, for example?'

Maree shook her head. 'Both Brooke and Patricia would have been working. There must have been some sudden and very important reason for coming. They couldn't have suspected they were coming into danger, or they would never have brought Cameron.'

She explained again about the balaclavas, and Brooke's belief that they thought Damien had somewhere concealed a significant quantity of drugs.

'They certainly wanted something they believed he had hidden, and they were desperate to get it.'

She paused as a thought hit her. 'Wait! What an idiot I am! Why didn't I think of that before? When we all came out here to get a rose for Mr Martin, Cameron was exploring and saw a van parked in the barn — you could see through cracks in the weatherboards. The door had a chain and padlock on it then. They're not there now. I wonder if Brooke or Pat suddenly began to wonder whether the van — or rather something in it — was what the thugs wanted, and they came out here to look, and ran into them?'

The police-officers still looked doubtful, but Tom was already opening the doors. 'It's not here now,' he said.

One of the officers bent down to look at the ground. 'A vehicle has certainly been driven out of here very recently — since that shower this morning.' There was mounting interest in his voice.

His colleague was walking back towards the gate. 'There's a different set of tracks here, showing where another vehicle has come in, turned around and gone out again,' he said.

'Get on the radio,' the senior constable said briskly. 'Probable abduction, two vehicles involved, probably heading south towards Brisbane, one believed to be a white van.' He looked at Maree. 'Make?'

She shook her head. 'It didn't seem to matter when I saw it. Just a white panel van, maybe about a tonne capacity, old, but in reasonable condition.'

They left Constable Bellingham to call the station and went into the barn. Clear in the dust on the floor were footprints.

'Careful not to walk over those,' Redford said. 'They might be useful. Two sets of boot-prints, see? Different tread-marks. Men's boots, by the size. And one set of small ones — a child's.'

Tom put a hand on Maree's shoulder,

knowing they were both seeing a similar picture: Cameron, full of curiosity, going into the barn and stumbling on two men who had had no hesitation in seizing him, his mother and Brooke, in order to avoid having their plans foiled, whatever those plans might have been. Desperate men who might very well resort to murder in order to cover their tracks. He wanted to scream at the police to move, to give chase. But the senior constable was still studying the floor.

'These,' he said, picking up some pale, rounded pellets. 'They look as if they're freshly dropped, probably from the van.'

He rubbed a couple between his fingers, sniffed them, touched one with his tongue and spat in disgust.

'They're just fertilizer,' he said. 'I'm a farm boy,' he added by way of explanation. 'It's certainly not drugs.'

'But there must be some significance in the van,' Tom said. 'All right, maybe it had fertilizer in it. But that might just have been cover for something else, mightn't it?'

'Granted,' the policeman agreed. He looked at Maree, and for the first time both she and Tom realized that for all his methodical calmness, the officer was intensely concerned. 'Is there anything, anything at all, that you can remember about the van that might help identify it? You understand there are hundreds of white panel vans on the road.'

Maree shook her head. 'I can't think — I didn't take any real notice, that day. It was just a white van parked in a locked shed. There wasn't any reason any of us should have taken any special notice.'

She frowned. 'Wait. There was something. Something I noticed. Oh, God, I can't remember. Some mark — a dent or something. I'd recognize it if I saw it, though, I'm sure.'

'Was there anything written on it — a company name, company logo?'

'No. I'm sure of that. It was just a plain, unmarked van. I took it for granted — we all did — that either it belonged to old Mr Martin and he wouldn't sell it, or it belonged to the next-door farmer and he just parked it here. And either way the shed was locked for security.'

'Brian,' the senior constable said, 'take the car, go check the neighbours out about the van — is it theirs. I'll radio in for someone to come out and check everything here and secure the area so nothing's disturbed. Then I'll wait here with these people till you get back. Make it quick.'

'We could be following those creeps in my

car,' Tom said urgently. 'If Maree can identify the van — '

'No.' The officer was bluntly direct. 'We don't know yet that the van was involved. We may need Miss Stewart's help. But we have to eliminate the possibility that the van belongs to the neighbouring farmer and has no connection with what's happened.'

The senior made his call to his station. The constable drove away. They waited, and while they waited Senior Constable Redford walked carefully around the shed, searching through the long grass and weeds, finding nothing.

It seemed like hours. It was perhaps six minutes.

The constable came back, driving fast. 'The farmer doesn't own the van. He doesn't lease this area where the sheds are. He doesn't know anything about the van, except he says the shed was unlocked and empty six months ago, because he was working nearby one day when a thunderstorm came up and he took shelter in the shed.'

'Right. I'll call the boss. At least we know now we're definitely looking for a white van which may be headed for Brisbane. Whether or not the missing people are in it or in the other vehicle is anybody's guess.'

'Sounds as though the proverbial needle in the haystack would be a lot easier to find,' the constable said wryly.

'But there can't be all that many white panel vans travelling between here and Brisbane,' Maree protested.

'Whoever took your friends away allowed Mrs Hardwick to make that phonecall,' the constable said quietly. 'They might have chosen to give her false information about their destination so she couldn't leave any clues.'

'Oh,' Maree said bleakly. 'Yes. I hadn't thought of that.' She put a hand to her head. 'Why can't I remember what was distinctive about that van? It wasn't much — nothing glaringly obvious like a non-matching door or anything like that.'

The senior constable finished speaking on the radio.

'The inspector has ordered a helicopter for aerial surveillance of all roads in the area, looking for a white van with another vehicle appearing to be travelling with it. Patrols will be out to stop all unmarked white vans.'

He looked at Maree. 'We're ordered to follow the apparent route the van would have taken — highway towards Brisbane. I'm authorized to take you with us in the hope you can spot the suspect vehicle. You also, sir,' he added to Tom, 'if you both agree.'

'Oh, for God's sake, of course we agree,' Tom said. 'Let's go.'

Back in the Sunshine Coast station the detective inspector who was now co-ordinating the operation at that end said with the grim practicality born of a long career of meeting human evil, 'Even if the abductors are headed for Brisbane, are they going to put up with the inconvenience of three passengers for the whole distance? Even if those people are alive now, my guess is they'll be taken along some side-road and disposed of. Whatever's going on, they're only an encumbrance. If any of you is a praying person, better start praying the chopper spots that van heading up a forestry-track somewhere. And while you're at it, pray it's not just dead bodies they're going to dispose of.'

A policewoman tapped on the open office door. 'Sir, Eric Redford just called in. Miss Stewart, who's travelling with them, says Mrs Hardwick made a deliberate reference to the New Day community during that phonecall. Miss Stewart says it made no sense at face value, so it must have been meant to direct attention there.'

'New Day.' The inspector frowned. 'Aren't they that alternative life style group — sort of retreat for addicts?'

263

'That's right.' Detective Sergeant Harold Thorpe spoke up.

'Know anything about them? Apart from rumour, I mean?'

'I'd swear they'd have nothing to do with kidnapping. They're a pretty genuine lot, as far as I can see. They provide a retreat for anyone who wants to get away from the world for a while. They don't pretend to work any kind of miracles or anything like that. They're pretty down to earth.'

'That's not to say they don't attract some kink-heads,' the inspector said. 'You and David get down there and check them out over this. You've had dealings with Mrs Hardwick.' He looked alertly at Harold Thorpe. 'What do you think of the theory that she was giving hidden clues in that phonecall? Is she smart enough?'

'She's smart enough,' the detective sergeant said.

* * *

In the speeding police car, with Constable Bellingham driving, Maree looked at Tom Alford. His face was pale, and tense jaw muscles told his teeth were clenched. Maree didn't voice her thoughts, but she suspected his were the same: Brooke and Patricia and

Cameron had been taken away, beyond doubt. But had they been alive? Dead bodies were much less trouble. And if they'd been taken away alive, how long before their captors sought some nice remote spot to dispose of them? The possible manner of that disposal was best not thought about. If one could avoid thinking.

* * *

The heat in the back of the van was stifling. Brooke tried constantly to fight the heavy tape that bound her wrists and ankles, but the effort was exhausting and she was drenched in sweat. And the tapes were totally unyielding. Donald had not relied on their adhesive qualities, but had tied them as if they were rope.

The heat and the enclosed space accentuated the heavy smell of the diesel fuel that had been poured into the bag of fertilizer. She had a hideous fear that any or all of them might become nauseated by the heat and the smell. To vomit with the gags in place meant to choke. At least instant death when the lethal van-load exploded would be infinitely preferable.

From time to time she turned her head to meet Patricia's eyes, but mostly Patricia

265

watched her son. Cameron had fought valiantly against his bonds, but with the same total lack of success. Now he sat with his eyes closed some of the time, as if he were thinking desperately of some plan of action.

Brooke felt swamped with love and admiration for her companions. Neither of them showed panic, nor any trace of the paralysing terror they must feel.

She wondered whether either of them had thought that they might after all be considered too much of a risk to take all the way. There were plenty of side-roads, especially into plantations of pine-forests, where they might be taken and disposed of, safely out of sight and hearing of anyone. Only Donald's fear of witnessing violence had kept them alive this far.

If the van slowed and made a distinct turn, and the smoothness of sealed road gave way to gravel, they would know they were not going to live to reach Brisbane.

They would be, she reflected bitterly, only a very small part of the carnage that would strike unsuspecting, innocent people, in probably not more than an hour and a half from now. People in a hotel, Donald had said. Which hotel, and why, she didn't know.

This was the 'monstrous evil' that had driven Rachel Hardwick to kill the son she adored. This was the hideous crime that had been planned, somewhere in his twisted mind, by the man Brooke had once been in love with. The brilliant, handsome, laughing, charming madman.

Rachel had known. He had told her, so certain that what he planned was right, and praiseworthy. But he had not told Rachel that he had accomplices. Rachel had not known that destroying Damien did not destroy the plan.

Brooke thought of Tom, so different. Quieter, gentler, ordinary looking. And if she had been given the chance to live another sixty years, she would have loved him for all of them. Now he would never know. She had tried to say to Maree, at the end of that phonecall, 'Tell Tom I love him'. But Donald had snatched the phone away.

Maree had understood a great deal of that call. Perhaps she had guessed that, as well.

But there was no possible way anyone could guess the reason for the abduction; no way to know if the van was involved, and no way to know it was a mobile bomb timed to explode in less than two hours. There had been no chance for her to warn Maree of that. At the first hint of such a warning Donald would have shut the phone off. All anyone could hope for now was that the police, in following up such meagre clues as she had been able to give, might possibly trace Donald and Jack through the New Day community, and end their madness.

The explosion might leave enough bits of the van for police to begin to link the two crimes. That was the only hope left; not that she and Patricia and Cameron could survive, but that these evil men could be caught before they struck again.

She wondered what drove them to want to do this. Donald had a haunted look, as though some tragedy in his past had tipped him over the edge of reason, much as had happened with Damien. Jack — Jack, she felt, was different. Whatever demons drove him, it was the prospect of killing that excited Jack. He, she felt, would kill for pleasure. Jack hated all the world. Whatever it was that had happened to him in the past, he blamed all of humanity for it.

Her body ached badly from being bound, doubled up in a position that had immediately been uncomfortable. By journey's end they would all be in agony from cramp. At least death would end that.

The road beneath the van was still smooth bitumen.

11

'Looks a peaceful enough place,' Detective Hanson commented as they drove into the New Day settlement. 'Almost a little village.'

A sun-tanned, shirtless young man in navy shorts and boots was parking a tractor in a shed; a handful of children were still splashing in the swimming-pool, overseen by two young women, who were urging them to come out, it was tea-time; an elderly man was walking with his dog; smells of evening meals being cooked wafted from cottages.

A few curious glances greeted the detectives as they got out of their unmarked car beside the sign which said 'Office'. A tall man came to the door, looking slightly surprised.

'Good-evening,' he said. 'I'm George Macintosh. How can I help you?'

The detectives identified themselves and he asked them into the office, where a young woman of Asian appearance was typing. When they were seated he looked at them expectantly.

'Is something wrong?'

'Just a routine inquiry,' Sergeant Thorpe said, settled back in his chair with his customary watchful stillness. 'How many vehicles belong on this property?'

George Macintosh raised his eyebrows slightly. 'A minibus takes the children to and from school, there is a Toyota Landcruiser pick-up truck for farm-work, I personally own an elderly Ford Laser sedan, and there is a tractor. Those are the actual permanent community vehicles. Of course, some of the residents own their own private vehicles.'

'Can you tell me exactly how many, and what the vehicles are?'

George Macintosh frowned slightly. 'People come and go here, you know,' he said mildly, 'though some have been here for several years. Others may come for only a few weeks — less, sometimes, depending on their own circumstances and whether or not this life suits them. But let me see. I think there are four private cars here at the moment, and one motor bike.'

He ticked them off on his fingers. 'A blue Mazda three-two-three, fairly old. A silver Hyundai Lantra, quite new; a white Holden Commodore station-wagon, and a white Ford Falcon sedan. The motor bike is, a Yamaha.'

'That's all?'

'Yes, I'm sure. As I say, people come and go, but there haven't been any new arrivals or departures recently. They're the only vehicles, aren't they, Helen?' He appealed to the typist.

'Yes,' she said, turning her head to look at the men. 'They're the only ones I can think of.' She went back to typing.

'Are all the vehicles here at the moment?' Thorpe asked.

'Probably. You see, some people go out to work from here — it's not an enclosed community or anything like that. But I guess everyone's likely to be back by now. It's nearly six-thirty. Oh, one car won't be here yet — Jack Walters's white Falcon. He and Donald Roberts work together — they're in insurance — and they said this morning they had to see a client in Brisbane and it was a late appointment, so they'd be very late back. But come, we'll check the others, if you like.'

All were duly accounted for.

'This vehicle that's still away — a white Ford Falcon, I think you said — who did you say owned it?' Thorpe asked.

'Jack Walters.' George Macintosh looked hard at the sergeant. 'Is there a problem? Is Jack in trouble?'

'Oh, we have no reason to think so,' Harold Thorpe said calmly. 'Is he likely to be?'

The older man hesitated thoughtfully. 'I shouldn't think so. Jack was a very disturbed man when he came here, and I was uneasy over whether our community was right for

271

him. I know little about him — I don't pry into people's problems. They tell me what they want to tell. I gather he came from a family where there was a very abusive alcoholic father. Jack was bitter. But he struck up a friendship with Donald Roberts, who got him this insurance job, and he has seemed vastly happier.'

'Do you happen to know the registration number of his car?'

Brother George shook his head, concern in his eyes. 'I'm afraid I've no idea — I fancy there's a letter K in it. I would tell you if I knew it. And I wish I knew why you're asking.'

'We're simply eliminating possibilities.'

'Do you get many visitors?' Detective Hanson asked casually. 'People dropping in out of curiosity, for instance?'

George Macintosh smiled. 'Some, yes. Mainly convinced we're up to no good. None in the past couple of weeks, though. Is that why you're here also?'

'No, not at all,' David Hanson said cheerfully. 'Just a routine motor vehicle check concerning another matter. Thanks very much for your time.'

They walked back to their car and the girl who had been typing in the office came over to them with a smile.

'Excuse me, may I show you a little of our farm? I work on it most of the time — I only help in the office sometimes because I'm used to that work. But I am so proud of the farm. You would find it interesting.'

As the detectives were getting into their car and were clearly anything but interested, she dropped her voice to a whisper. 'Please,' she urged. 'It's important. Something may be very wrong here.'

They hesitated. 'Oh,' Harold Thorpe said a shade impatiently, 'all right. I guess we can spare a few minutes.'

'Oh, good!' she said eagerly. 'Down by the dam we have ducklings, and two wild black swans are nesting. And we have two very special new calves, born just last night.'

She was walking briskly off as she spoke, and the detectives exchanged slightly despairing glances, but followed.

They obediently looked where she pointed at calves and ducklings while, safely out of earshot of everyone else, the girl said urgently, 'I don't know why you're here, and I didn't want to say anything in front of Brother George — George Macintosh — because it would seem strange that I didn't speak up before. I'm sure Brother George didn't think it mattered, and so didn't mention it, because it happened some time

273

ago. When I first came here, about six months ago, there was another vehicle that belonged here. A white van. I don't know the make.'

She didn't seem to notice their sharpened interest. 'It was supposed to have been stolen shortly after I came here, but I'm certain it wasn't. Or at least not in the way everyone was told. Brother George reported it, of course. He had no reason to doubt it had been stolen. But it was never found.'

The detectives were watching her alertly now.

'Jack Walters and Donald Roberts were supposed to have taken the van to Brisbane to get parts for the tractor here. They came back in a taxi, saying they had parked the van in the car-park of a Brisbane hotel while they had lunch, and when they came out it was gone, and they'd had to come home by train and taxi.'

Sergeant Thorpe was watching her expressionlessly. 'And?'

'I had driven to the shopping centre in Maroochydore that day to buy blankets. My car is the old blue Mazda. Jack and Donald hadn't gone to Brisbane. They were there, in the shopping centre car-park. We are not bad people here,' she said earnestly. 'The place is not a cover-up for a bunch of crazies. We are just people working through

274

problems. But something is wrong about those two — Donald and Jack. I don't know what it is, but something. I am fairly sure no one else here is involved in whatever it is with them.'

'So — Helen, isn't it?' Detective Hanson said. 'They didn't go to Brisbane as they were supposed to. But the van might still have been stolen — in Maroochydore instead of Brisbane.'

Helen shook her head. 'No one stole it from them. When I saw them they were talking to another man. I'd seen him before. He'd been here several times, and they were friendly with him, so I thought maybe they'd just taken some time off to have lunch together or something. Then they gave him the keys to the van and he unlocked it and got in and drove away and they just walked off. I didn't take any more notice and didn't think of it again for days, and then I heard that the van had been stolen. But it wasn't. They simply let that man take it away.'

'Why didn't you say something to George Macintosh? Or the two men?'

'I was new here. I had — some problems of my own. And I was afraid of Jack Walters.'

'Why were you afraid?'

She hesitated, and then said slowly, 'Because of the feeling that those two men are different. Something about them is wrong.'

'In what way?' If Sergeant Thorpe felt the young woman was wasting his time, he gave no sign of it.

'Donald Roberts is fanatically opposed to drug use. To be opposed is not unusual, and perfectly reasonable and sensible. But not like that. He is fanatical. And Jack Walters asked me once if I was Cambodian.'

'Why? Are you?'

'No. Filipino. I asked him why he wanted to know, because he seemed really disappointed. He said he thought I might have seen some of the massacres in Pol Pot's time.'

She shivered. 'He said he'd always wondered what it would be like to kill a lot of people. He seemed excited, and then he said: 'Maybe I'll find out one day'. He frightened me. Other times he seemed just ordinary.'

'People sometimes say stupid things to deliberately frighten someone,' David Hanson said soothingly. 'Did you know the man who took the van? You say he'd been here?'

'Only to visit. I don't remember his name, but I think he was a priest or something. He was murdered soon after.'

'Damien Hardwick,' Detective Hanson said softly.

'Hardwick — yes!' Helen said. 'Donald and Jack were very distressed when he was killed.

More than I would have thought if they didn't know each other very well.'

Both policemen were watching her intently now. 'In what way were they upset?' the sergeant asked. 'Grieving? Angry?'

Helen considered for a second. 'Both of those things. I heard them talking one day when they didn't know I was near. I remember almost exactly what they said, because they frightened me. Jack said: 'The bitch must have found out. He said she'd kill him rather than let him go on with it'. And Donald said: 'We have to find it. We can still do this. It's God's work. He told us he'd been told by God to do it. We know what to do once we find the stuff. It was a terrible mistake for him not to tell us where it is, even though he believed the fewer people who knew of it the safer the secret was. But the evil creature must be destroyed'.'

There was a little silence. Then David Hanson said, 'The evil creature. Did he mean a person?'

'Oh, yes, I think so.'

'The woman? The one they called the bitch?'

'I don't think so,' Helen said slowly, 'because to destroy this person they had to *find* something. That's what they said. Find *it*, they said, not find *her*.'

'And you've no idea who this evil creature might be?'

She shook her head. 'No. Although . . . ' she stopped frowning. 'Donald has often spoken with much bitterness about some American who wants free drugs given to addicts. Whether that's the one they called the evil creature, I don't know.'

'And Hardwick said he'd been told by God to do something which Jack and Donald now plan to do,' Harold Thorpe said musingly, as if thinking aloud. 'And they apparently gave Hardwick a white van.'

The two detectives looked at each other.

'Told by God,' Detective Hanson repeated. 'What was it Damien Hardwick's mother wrote? Something about there being nothing more dangerous than someone who believes he's been told by God to do violence. What if we've been wrong, and it wasn't his wife Hardwick was planning to kill? Isn't that American doctor going to lecture in Brisbane? That fellow who wants free drugs handed out to addicts? When is he due to give his lecture?'

'Tonight,' the sergeant said. He wheeled around to look at the girl. 'That van — do you know the make of it? The number?'

She shook her head. 'Brother George should know, if you ask.'

'We'll talk to him.' The two men turned together and began to run back to their car. 'Thank you!' the sergeant said over his shoulder. 'Thank you very much.'

'I haven't wasted your time too much?' she called after them anxiously.

'No!' David Hanson called back. 'Although,' he muttered, 'I hope it was a waste of time. I hope.'

'And we'd better keep hoping,' Harold Thorpe said grimly as he reached for the two-way radio. 'I've seldom been more anxious to be made to look like a fool. But Brooke Hardwick makes a phonecall full of double meanings, then she and her friends vanish and so does a white van, and she takes care to mention this community and the fact that she and the others are going to Brisbane. And two possibly kinked men who gave Hardwick a white van that wasn't theirs to give are missing from this community. Somewhere around where that doctor's lecture is being held somebody'd better start looking for a white van. Fast.'

12

At the Brisbane end of the investigation Detective Inspector Clark turned from the radio to the policewoman who had called him to take the message from Harold Thorpe. 'Check vehicle records for a van — make unknown — reported stolen about six months ago by a George Macintosh. Get make and number. And the registration number of a white Falcon sedan owned by a Jack — probably John — Walters.'

He looked at a uniformed constable. 'Any word from that helicopter?'

The man turned from his radio. 'They've spotted eleven white vans, unmarked, on the highway. They're all being stopped as they reach the parked patrol cars. Three vans on side-roads have not yet been intercepted. No obvious indication of an accompanying vehicle, though pretty much impossible to tell on the highway, and two on side-roads have vehicles not far behind them.'

'They're to be kept under surveillance.' He turned to a constable. 'That American pro-free-drugs doctor who's to speak in Brisbane tonight. Get me the venue and the time. And get him on the phone. I need to talk to him if he hasn't left for the lecture venue. He may be the target of an assassination attempt. Relay that information to the patrol car that's in pursuit of the van and has the civilian who claims she can identify the van on sight. Inform them the men they're after are probably armed and dangerous.'

He sat back and frowned. 'And what the hell they're armed with, we haven't a clue. Guns of some sort, most probably. But what? Mix with the crowd and use a hand-gun up close? Use a sniper's rifle from an upstairs window? Rush up with an AK Forty-seven and start blasting at random?'

The policewoman who had been checking vehicle records spoke. 'The vehicle as reported stolen from George Malcolm Macintosh was a white one-ton Ford Courier panel van, never located, but the registration plates were found a few days later in a rubbish-bin. So if it's on the road it's using false plates. Three Ford Falcon sedans are registered to owners named John Walters. These are the registration numbers.' She handed him a piece of paper.

'Right. Have these people's whereabouts checked and get these numbers out to all units, pronto.'

'Sir,' a constable said, 'Doctor Crawford, the fellow giving tonight's lecture, can't be contacted. He's on his way to the Crest of Gold Hotel — that's the venue for the meeting, but it's not the hotel where he's been staying.'

'Damn. When's the meeting due to start?'

'Seven-thirty. About thirty minutes from now.'

'Doctor Crawford is to be stopped the moment he arrives and urgently warned to leave immediately by a different route. What's the location of that pursuing patrol car?'

'Last reported on Lutwych Road, heading south still.'

'Tell them the venue. And some time, when this is over, get me the names of those officers, and the detectives who went to that community. They've done well.'

He buried his face in his hands for a second. 'And the whole thing may be a massive false alarm.'

'Sir,' a detective said urgently, 'a message has just come in from the pursuing patrol car. I think you should know.'

* * *

There had been little conversation in the patrol car as it raced through the fading

summer afternoon that was sliding impercep-
tibly into dusk, the upward-slanting rays of
sunlight gleaming on puffs of white cloud in a
sky of paling blue.

No one noticed it was a beautiful
afternoon.

Maree sat tensely, eyes glued on the
vehicles ahead. She had said once, with
infinite bitterness, 'Why can't I remember
what it was about that van that caught my
attention?'

Tom had said quietly, 'You'll remember if
we see it.'

She flicked a glance at him and said
quietly, 'Tom, right at the end of that
phonecall, Brooke said: 'Tell Tom'. But I'm
certain she was going to say more, and
someone snatched the phone away. I've a
feeling she was going to say: 'Tell Tom I love
him'.'

He said nothing for a string of seconds, and
then said very softly, 'Thank you, Maree. I
wish to God I'd told her I love her.'

From time to time the radio had crackled
to life, informatively or questioningly, and
had been answered by Senior Constable
Redford. Brian Bellingham drove the patrol
car — lights flashing, his concentration
intense — faster than Maree or Tom had ever
been driven before, as he desperately tried to

claw back some of the lead the van had.

If it had come this way at all.

Once they reached the suburbs and their criss-crossing maze of streets filled with traffic, the silence in the car became not concentration but despair.

Maree said finally, breaking the silence to give voice to all their thoughts, 'We'll never find them now. And they'll be dead, already, won't they? Those thugs would never bring them all this way alive.'

'We'll just keep on through the city, unless we're called off,' Eric Redford said, trying not to let his voice betray his hopelessness. 'It's worth a try.' They all knew he was lying.

An authoritative voice called the car through the radio, and when Redford acknowledged, said crisply, 'Suspects may be *en route* to Crest of Gold Hotel, Gregory Terrace. Possible attempt to assassinate a Doctor Crawford who is to address a seven-thirty gathering in the hotel convention-room. Suspects may be armed and dangerous.'

As Redford acknowledged, Constable Bellingham said, 'I know that hotel. My sister's wedding reception was held there.' He turned on the siren and trod on the accelerator, and Tom Alford sat bolt upright.

'Oh, God,' he breathed, and the anguish

that clawed inside him showed in his voice. 'Maybe I'm off-beam, but suddenly some senseless things make sense. The thugs who threatened Brooke demanded to know where 'the stuff' was. And where that van had been, we found freshly dropped pellets of fertilizer. There was a strong smell of diesel fuel in the barn. I assumed the van had a diesel motor. But I think the diesel had been added to the fertilizer, and the fertilizer was ammonium nitrate. Add a detonating device and the diesel-fertilizer mix becomes high explosive, doesn't it? I think that van's a mobile bomb. That's their assassination weapon.'

There was a moment of shocked silence, and then Eric Redford pressed the call button on his radio.

The car raced through, scattering evening traffic, the shriek and wail of its siren a familiar-enough sound in any city, but Constable Bellingham drove with unfamiliar desperation, weaving through traffic. As they tore past the great bulk of the Royal Brisbane Hospital, Maree wondered grimly how soon someone there would be told the hospital might soon need all its resources to deal with the multiple casualties of a disaster. And all its fine facilities would be of no use to many, if this chase was all too late.

Brian Bellingham swung into Gregory

Terrace against a red light and a fraction before a semi-trailer took them to oblivion, and in moments whipped the car in a screaming turn into the charmingly designed entrance to an imposing, multi-storeyed hotel.

There were no white vans in the car-park.

The constable turned the car down the side-drive toward the service area. There was only a fire-equipment service van. He turned again.

'We'll check the street,' he said. Other sirens were wailing closer.

'Stop!' Maree shouted. 'That's it!'

Tyres screeched in protest at the stop. Eric Redford looked at Maree. 'But it's a fire-equipment van. You said — '

'I know. They've painted it. That's it.' She was flinging open the door as Tom leapt out on the other side, and the policemen followed.

'Are you certain?' Redford demanded.

'Look.' Maree pointed to the panel just behind the driver's door. 'That rust-patch. It's an almost perfect map of South America.'

Eric Redford reached for the radio once more, and Brian Bellingham flicked open the car's boot and took out a wrecking-bar as Tom and Maree tried vainly to open the van's rear doors.

The policewoman who had been detailed to run vehicle checks spoke to Inspector Clark.

'Only one of the Ford Falcons registered to people named John Walters or Jack Walters is white. The registered owner was watching television in his living-room in Cairns and his car is in his garage. The suspect Walters must be using a false name, unless he's from interstate. That's being checked now.'

'The detectives who are at that commune are to search the suspect's room, particularly looking for a driving licence or any other documents in a different name. Search even if they have to break the door down, and to hell with search-warrants.'

'Sir.' She moved away with the unobtrusive briskness that pervaded the whole room as people went about their tasks.

A uniformed inspector appeared at Inspector Clark's elbow. 'Streets are being cordoned off and evacuation of the hotel and nearby buildings has been ordered. The bomb squad has been called. The commissioner was just leaving for dinner with friends. He's on his way to the scene.'

Chester Clark looked at his watch. 'And it's far too late to help anyone if the explosion happens to be timed for the start of the meeting. Or else it's a massive false alarm.'

The constable at the radio looked up. 'I don't think it's a false alarm, sir. They've found the van parked beside the hotel. No sign of the suspects. Constable Bellingham is forcing the rear doors of the van.'

The policewoman was back. 'The detectives had already begun to search Jack Walters's room, sir. They found a driving licence in the name of John Franklin Adams. He is the registered owner of a Ford Falcon sedan with this number.'

'Good work. Put out a call to all units. No one is to intercept, only follow, unless there are two persons in that car. I want them both. Then they must be approached with caution and not without other officers in attendance. Suspects are probably armed and dangerous. And I want them.'

He turned to the radio man, who shook his head. 'Nothing further about the van, sir. Bomb squad is on its way. Surrounding streets are being cordoned off and the hotel has begun evacuation.'

Chester Clark looked at his watch again, almost as if he could will the minute-hand to cease its remorseless sinking toward the figure six.

'It'll be a timed device with an electronic detonator. Everything depends on what time

288

is set on the clock. If it's set for the opening of the meeting, God help us all.'

★ ★ ★

Brian Bellingham was struggling to force the tip of the wrecking-bar around the edge of the tight-fitting door as Tom shouted, 'Brooke! Brooke, we're here!'

Above the wail of approaching sirens and the clamour of the fire alarm in the hotel urging people to flee, it was impossible to hear whether there was any faint response.

'It'll be a timer attached to an electronic detonator,' Eric Redford said beside them, trying futilely to fit his fingers under the double rear doors, unaware that he was echoing Inspector Clark's words. 'With a stick of gelignite, probably. Just a little bomb on its own. But when that little bomb blows, it'll instantly turn that fertilizer into a huge bomb.' He was panting with exertion and the desperate need for haste. 'And it'll be — you beauty!' he breathed as Brian's wrecking-bar found purchase between the doors, and the young constable used all his strength to wrench the doors open with a shriek of protesting metal.

'Brooke! Oh, Brooke! Don't say she's dead!' Tom Alford cried.

The three forms were huddled and still, each in an almost foetal position.

'Get them out!' Redford snapped at Tom. 'Brian, we've got to shift the bags!'

The two policemen leapt into the back of the van, stepping over the huddled forms, and began dragging apart the stack of heavy sacks of fertilizer.

'It'll probably be at the bottom,' Eric Redford panted.

Tom pulled Brooke into his arms and almost sobbed with relief as she moaned faintly. Maree lifted Cameron out, and both turned for Patricia. Cameron's eyes were open and alert, but his mother lay pale and dazed.

And they all knew that if the explosion came, none of them would survive. Tom pulled out a pocket-knife and carefully slid the blade under the tape where it was bound over the handkerchief across Brooke's mouth, while her eyes watched him dazedly. He cut carefully through the tape and eased it aside.

Eric Redford dumped a bag of fertilizer out of the van and shouted at him.

'Put them in the patrol car and go! Go!'

Understanding, Tom picked Brooke up and dumped her without ceremony on the back seat. Maree half dragged, half carried Cameron, and they both lifted Patricia. Then

Tom touched Maree on the shoulder.

'Drive away — far as you can get.'

'What about you?' Maree stared at him.

'I'm needed here. Go!' he shouted frantically.

'Tom.' Brooke's voice, so hoarse as to be almost beyond understanding, croaked.

He swung around.

She forced her voice to function. 'Seven-thirty.'

'Got it.' He flashed her a smile and turned to the van. Maree slipped in behind the wheel and started the car.

Tom scrambled in beside the two police-men. If the bomb's timer was accurate they had just over a minute. 'It's set for seven-thirty,' he told them, grabbing hold of a sack and dragging it backwards out of the van.

'I've got it.' Redford had the slit sack that had the corner of a box showing through the slit. Sweat was pouring down his face, but his hands were rock steady.

He frantically scooped some of the fertilizer out and pulled out a cardboard box. Cradling it in his arms he jumped from the van and ran across the car-park.

'Get down flat!' he shouted.

'Eric!' Tom screamed at him. '*Throw it! Now!*'

Then Brian Bellingham pulled him down to the floor of the van as a thunderous blast split the evening.

The van jolted in the shock wave and bits of debris rained down around them and they stood up shakily to see a mushrooming fireball, black-topped with smoke, rising above the car-park. The two men began running towards it as a fire-truck charged into the car-park and headed for the fire.

A car was burning fiercely as the firemen unrolled hoses and poured foam into the flames. And Senior Constable Eric Redford, blood streaming down his face from a cut which revealed white cheek-bone underneath, scrambled to his feet, picked up his cap, and brushed some of the dust from his uniform.

He grinned ruefully at his colleague and Tom. 'I tried to throw the bloody thing into that excavation on the other side of the car-park, and I lobbed it under somebody's Mercedes instead. I won't be his favourite copper.'

Tom impulsively flung his arms around the policeman in a quick bear-hug. 'God, man, I thought you were dead.' He shook his head. 'I guess I thought we were all dead. You were damn quick to find that bag with the box of tricks in it before it set the whole thing off in a blast hundreds of times bigger.'

Eric Redford put a hand to his face and then looked in surprise at the blood on his fingers. 'Didn't know I had that,' he said, and added, 'My dad used to tell me how they blasted rock or big tree-stumps by using that sort of set-up, before regulations became much tighter, only of course they never used anything this big. There are some advantages in being a country boy, you see.'

★   ★   ★

In a ward in the Royal Brisbane Hospital, Detective Inspector Chester Clark, accompanied by a young policewoman, sat between the beds occupied by Brooke and Patricia. Night had long since dropped its cooling mantle over a city which would wake tomorrow to a full realization that tragedy had almost torn brutally at its peace. A doctor had told the inspector that the women would remain overnight, though Cameron Evans, with the resilience of nine years of age, had been released after having the residual glue from the adhesive bindings cleaned off his skin. Tom Alford and Maree Stewart had taken him for a meal.

'His mother and Mrs Hardwick have no physical injuries,' the doctor had said. 'Shock, strained muscles and wrists rubbed raw from fighting their bonds, but no actual injuries. The emotional injuries will take a while to work out of their systems, but they'll be fine. They are both highly intelligent and emotionally strong people.'

The police-officers had listened quietly as Brooke and Patricia had told their story.

Brooke said with a shudder, 'I shouldn't have allowed the others to go out to that barn — should have gone to the police. I just felt that we didn't have anything concrete to base suspicions on. I felt no one would take us seriously. I almost killed all three of us.'

'Mrs Hardwick,' Chester Clark said gently, 'to be perfectly honest, I doubt if any police-officer would have taken you very seriously. Doubtless they would have investigated, but not with any urgency. When they arrived, they would have found the barn, or machinery shed, or whatever it is, empty, and would have attached no significance to it. You and your friends would have lived. But God knows how many would have died when that van blew up. Blame is the last thing that can be attached to you people. I have nothing but praise for everyone involved.'

He looked from one to the other. 'A great many people owe you and your friends and the on-the-spot police more than they can guess. Mrs Hardwick, one thing puzzles me.

It's unfortunately fairly simple to get information on how to build a bomb. But where would someone like your husband get the material he needed — a stick of gelignite and an electronic detonator? You can't just walk into a hardware store and buy them. There are very strict regulations.'

Brooke nodded. 'I thought a lot about that. In actual fact, I think it would have been quite easy for Damien to get the explosives just *because* of who he was. A member of his congregation was in charge of blasting operations at a local quarry. I remember actually hearing Damien expressing interest in his work. The man invited him to go out to the quarry and see it for himself. And even if, at the end of the day, anyone counted and found a stick of gelignite and a detonator not accounted for, who would suspect the charming young Anglican minister of pocketing them?'

The inspector nodded. 'I see the point.'

Patricia said, 'Inspector, Damien Hardwick has been dead for months. Why did he set up a bomb all that time before it was needed? There was always a chance it'd be discovered.'

'I think the explanation is quite simple. Doctor Crawford was scheduled to come to Australia last July, but his visit was postponed because he was seriously ill.'

A nurse tentatively parted the curtains at the foot of the beds. 'Excuse me, Inspector, but these ladies have some anxious visitors. May they come in?'

'Yes, certainly,' the inspector said. 'I've no more questions here at the moment.'

He stood up as Tom and Maree came in with Cameron. Somewhere they had found a shop where they had bought him a set of new clothes to replace the ones he had been wearing, thoroughly filthy from the dusty sacks in the barn and dust and fertilizer on the floor of the van. He hesitated for a second, awed momentarily by the hospital atmosphere, then when Patricia smiled and held out her arms he skipped across and hugged her massively.

'Hey!' he said. 'They've cut your hair.'

'That was to get rid of the glue from the sticky tape,' Patricia told him. 'One of the nurses did it. Brooke's, too. I think she did pretty well as a hairdresser, don't you?'

'Uh-huh.' He nodded. 'Looks good.' He turned to Brooke. 'Are you okay, Brooke?'

'Fine,' she smiled, holding Tom's hand as he sat beside her.

'You know,' Cameron said seriously, 'it'd be nice if you married Mr Alford.'

'Well,' Brooke said, eyes twinkling, 'Mr

Alford would have to think so, too.'

'Oh, he does. I asked him earlier.'

For the first time in a good many hours that seemed like half a lifetime, they all laughed.

Cameron, totally unabashed, turned to Maree. 'Maree, I forgot to ask you: you drove us away from the bomb, didn't you? In the police car?'

'Well, only a little way,' Maree said. 'I'd only just got out into the street when the bomb went off, and I ran back, because . . . ' She stopped, and the laughter that had been in her face died, and she didn't finish the sentence — because I thought those three men must all be dead.

Cameron's train of thought was not about to be shunted aside. 'Was it exciting to drive the police car?'

'It was jolly good,' Maree said, smiling again, 'because I left it double-parked in the street, and I reckoned no one would ever give it a parking-ticket.'

He grinned delightedly, and the laughter was restored to the room.

'Guess what, Mum,' he said, fishing in the pocket of his new jeans.

Patricia smiled at him. 'What, darling?'

'The policeman who got his face cut gave me this while the ambulance people were cutting the tapes off us.' He held up a fragment of scorched metal which doubtless had once been part of a Mercedes. 'It came from the explosion. He said I could keep it as a souvenir. Do you think it might be part of the bomb, sir?' he asked the inspector hopefully.

Inspector Clark examined it solemnly. 'It could be,' he lied. 'It'll certainly send the other kids at your school wild with envy.'

'It will, won't it?' Cameron said happily. Then he frowned thoughtfully. 'Sir, how do you defuse a bomb?'

'Very carefully,' Chester Clark said feelingly. 'But I don't know much about it, because I'm not brave enough to be part of the bomb squad.'

'Oh, I bet you're brave as anything,' Cameron objected generously. 'What about the policeman who gave me this? Is he part of the bomb squad?'

'No. He's just a very brave young man who was part of a very brave team.'

His mobile phone buzzed and he answered it, and listened with a set face. 'Right,' he said. 'Thanks, Bruno. I'll be back at the station in half an hour.'

He switched the phone off and stood very still for a few seconds. Then he looked at Patricia and Brooke. 'I'm not sure whether you need any more talk of the men who abducted you, but you have more right than most to know. One of our patrol cars spotted their car and followed it. They evidently realized they were being followed and turned up a side-road. When our fellows followed, they must have known something had gone very wrong, and tried to outrun the patrol car. The driver lost control on a bend that evidently was sharper than he expected. The vehicle left the road and hit a tree. Neither of the abductors survived.'

He paused. 'They were always doomed, I think. Probably, whether or not they'd been foiled over the horror they had planned for tonight, they'd have tried another outrage. But the support they believed in wouldn't have happened. There'd have been no world-wide organization. Their warped dreams were never going to be any more than that: warped dreams.'

Into the silence that followed, the nurse returned, smiling. 'I have a frantically anxious gentleman at the desk who has just driven — at highly illegal speed, I suspect — from the Sunshine Coast. He says he heard of a kidnap on his car radio on his way home from the dentist, got home to find his fiancée missing, and has since been haunting the police until they could tell him where he might find a Maree Stewart. Is that you?' she asked Maree.

Maree's face lit joyfully. 'It's Harley!'

'Thank goodness. I can bring him in before he tears the place apart.'

She went out, laughing, and a few moments later Harley strode in and caught Maree wordlessly in his arms. She put her face against him, and for the first time the anguish of the past hours let go its grip, and she began to cry.

'Oh, Hal,' she said chokingly. 'I'm so glad you're here.'

Brooke and Tom looked at each other and smiled, and Tom bent and kissed her gently.

'If I remember rightly,' he said, 'this seems to be where we came in.'

THE END

We do hope that you have enjoyed reading this large print book.

Did you know that all of our titles are available for purchase?

We publish a wide range of high quality large print books including:
Romances, Mysteries, Classics
General Fiction
Non Fiction and Westerns

Special interest titles available in large print are:
The Little Oxford Dictionary
Music Book
Song Book
Hymn Book
Service Book

Also available from us courtesy of Oxford University Press:
Young Readers' Dictionary
(large print edition)
Young Readers' Thesaurus
(large print edition)

For further information or a free brochure, please contact us at:
Ulverscroft Large Print Books Ltd.,
The Green, Bradgate Road, Anstey,
Leicester, LE7 7FU, England.
Tel: (00 44) **0116 236 4325**
Fax: (00 44) **0116 234 0205**

Other titles in the
Ulverscroft Large Print Series:

STRANGER IN THE PLACE

Anne Doughty

Elizabeth Stewart, a Belfast student and only daughter of hardline Protestant parents, sets out on a study visit to the remote west coast of Ireland. Delighted as she is by the beauty of her new surroundings and the small community which welcomes her, she soon discovers she has more to learn than the details of the old country way of life. She comes to reappraise so much that is slighted and dismissed by her family — not least in regard to herself. But it is her relationship with a much older, Catholic man, Patrick Delargy, which compels her to decide what kind of life she really wants.

A GOOD MAN'S LOVE

Elizabeth Harris

Hal Dillon and Ben MacAllister had been deeply affected by the appalling death of their university friend Laurie. Hal journeyed to Mexico to continue his anthropological studies, and there found distraction in his passionate affair with Magdalena. But was he inviting even more heartache? Ben became a wanderer. While working in Cyprus he had met English girl Jo Daniel, and, after a nomadic summer together, they travelled to England to embark on what promised to be a lifetime of marital bliss. But Jo discovers that promises don't always come true.

SAFFRON'S WAR

Frederick E. Smith

Corporal Alan Saffron, ex-aircrew, is desperate to get back into action, but instead he's posted to Cape Town as an instructor, along with Ken Bickers, a friend about as hazardous as an enemy sniper, who considers Saffron a jonah for trouble. Within half an hour of arrival, Saffron's jonah strikes, and he makes an enemy of Warrant Officer Kruger, who turns Saffron's cushy posting into total warfare. With recruits as wild as Hottentots, obsolete aircraft, and Cape Town's infamous watch dog, Nuisance, Saffron's sojourn in South Africa becomes a mixture of adventure, danger and pure hilarity . . .

THE DEVIL'S BRIDE

Penelope Stratton

Lord Rupert Glennister's luck at cards and his tireless sexual appetites were thought to be the work of satanic forces. An outraged society made him an outcast until he could redeem himself by marrying a woman of virtue. Calvina Bracewell was a parson's daughter but was bullied into servitude by her 'benefactors'. Rescued by Lord Rupert, she found herself agreeing to his shocking demand that they should marry that very night. For a while, Calvina was happy but then attempts on her life began. Only one man could want her dead, and that was the husband she'd grown to love.

THE SURGEON'S APPRENTICE

Arthur Young

1947: Young Neil Aitken has worked hard to secure a place at Glasgow University to study medicine. Bearing in mind the Dean's warning that it takes more than book-learning to become a doctor, he sets out to discover what that other elusive quality might be. He learns the hard way, from a host of memorable characters ranging from a tyrannical surgeon to the bully on the farm where Neil works in his spare time, and assorted patients who teach him about courage and vulnerability. Neil also meets Sister Annie, the woman who is to influence his life in every way.